Penguin Books

The Pale Companion

Andrew Motion was born in London in 1952 and educated at University College, Oxford. He was a lecturer in English at the University of Hull from 1977 to 1981 and has been Editor of *Poetry Review*. He has published five books of poetry, *The Pleasure Steamers* (1978), *Independence* (1981), *Secret Narratives, Dangerous Play* (1984), winner of the Rhys Memorial Prize, and his latest collection, *Natural Causes* (1987); two critical studies, *The Poetry of Edward Thomas* (1978) and *Philip Larkin* (1982); and a biography of the Lamberts (1987). In 1981 he won the Arvon/*Observer* Poetry Prize and in 1987 the Somerset Maugham Award and the Dylan Thomas Award. He lives in London with his wife and their three children. *The Pale Companion* is his first novel.

THE PALE COMPANION

Andrew Motion

PENGUIN BOOKS

PENGUIN BOOKS

Published by the Penguin Group
Penguin Books Ltd, 27 Wrights Lane, London W8 5TZ, England
Viking Penguin, a division of Penguin Books USA Inc.
375 Hudson Street, New York, New York 10014, USA
Penguin Books Australia Ltd, Ringwood, Victoria, Australia
Penguin Books Canada Ltd, 2801 John Street, Markham, Ontario, Canada L3R 1B4
Penguin Books (NZ) Ltd, 182–190 Wairau Road, Auckland 10, New Zealand

Penguin Books Ltd, Registered Offices: Harmondsworth, Middlesex, England

First published by Viking 1989
Published in Penguin Books 1990
10 9 8 7 6 5 4 3 2 1

Printed in England by Clays Ltd, St Ives plc

For Jan Dalley

THESEUS: Go, Philostrate,
Stir up the Athenian youth to merriments.
Awake the pert and nimble spirit of mirth.
Turn melancholy forth to funerals:
The pale companion is not for our pomp.

A Midsummer Night's Dream, Act I, Scene 1

Chapter 1

A young dog fox trotted over the playing fields towards a massive, red-brick tower. It was a gatehouse, but the fox slipped through unnoticed, crossed a square lawn and came to the mouth of a long corridor. Hundreds of pieces of paper were pinned along one wall; parcels of dusty sunlight leant against the other. From the far end came a blank roar.

The fox slid nearer and the noise grew more complicated. There were squeals, yelps, tingling clashes. Then something slammed, heavy doors swung open and a bald man strode out with his hands behind his back. Other men followed in pairs, wearing gowns which bounced and fluttered.

'Look at that!' The bald man's voice cracked down the corridor.

Another voice, lighter, asked: 'What? Where?'

A finger pointed and the fox disappeared. 'You missed it. Dirty great ginger tom. Must have come up from the village.'

The men flapped out into a quadrangle and went their separate ways through the brilliant afternoon.

Hundreds of boys poured into the corridor, and the hundreds of pieces of paper panicked on the wall. Couples were jostled apart, knots of friends untied.

'Sod this,' Francis muttered. 'Jamie? Come on.'

A white face swung after him through a Gothic side door. 'Fucking hell.' Jamie brushed his lapels, peering down his bony nose. His voice was arch and metallic. 'I mean – what *is* the point?'

They were in a small courtyard roofed with the leaves of a sycamore growing in the centre.

1

'You're not rushing, are you?' asked Francis.

'Nothing that can't wait. What about you?'

They strolled in a slow circle, Jamie the taller and darker of the two, his head lurching a little with each step, like a camel's.

'Oh, you know,' Francis shrugged. The air was stagnant under the thick tree-ceiling, and as the racket of boys faded he could hear other smaller noises: a fly buzzing against a gluey leaf; the creak of high branches.

Jamie raised his fists and flicked out a few gangling punches. 'Float like a butterfly, sting like a bee, I am the greatest, God bless me.'

'What's that supposed to mean?'

'Boxing.'

'Your little friend?' Francis smoothed his fringe across his forehead.

'He's not little.' Jamie pretended to be hurt. 'And there's no need to sound like nanny.'

'I'm not.'

'You are.' Jamie stared up into the sycamore; the insides of his nostrils were raw and hairless. 'The usual for you, I suppose?'

'You know Keith and I've got a lot to do.'

'I do?'

Francis nodded sharply. 'Yes, you bloody do.'

They had come to a standstill. 'Are we going to have a tiff?' Jamie dabbed the pale mole on his cheek.

'No, Jamie.' Francis gritted his teeth. 'We are not going to have a tiff.'

'That's good, then.'

'You're just jealous.'

'I'm not jealous, in fact.'

'You are. You don't like him because I went off with him.'

'It's not the going off I mind . . . Just look out for him, that's all.' Jamie's mouth twitched. 'There's something about him, I . . .'

2

'This is your friendly advice, is it?' Francis interrupted. 'Well, thanks. You don't fancy him, that's all it is.'

'I couldn't give a fuck about fancying him. If you want swarthy Greeks . . .'

'He's not a swarthy Greek.' Francis flared up, then suddenly felt ridiculous and laughed. 'His mother's Greek. That's all.'

'Swarthyette, then.' Jamie slapped his brow. 'How should I know?' Their irritation melted. The sycamore groaned above them, and slabs of light slipped across their faces.

Francis rubbed him on the arm affectionately. 'Come on. People will start talking.'

Jamie led the way down the covered corridor. An older boy was standing by the door into the quadrangle, his gown slung across his shoulder.

'Look at Middleton,' whispered Jamie. 'The winnet.'

'Middleton. The only man in England with pubic hair on his head.'

'Elecktrickle banana,' Francis sang softly.

'Mayne!'

Francis shielded his eyes from the sun.

'Mayne, come here. And you, Jamieson. Both of you come here.' Middleton was pointing at the ground in front of him as if summoning a dog to heel. His furiously curly blond hair was plastered with oil and gleamed like a helmet. 'What are you two plotting?'

Francis looked at Jamie, wide-eyed and baffled. 'Nothing, Middleton. Did it look as though we were, Middleton? We were just talking.'

'That's right, Middleton. Just talking.'

'You're always smirking together, you two. It's not liked.'

'No, Middleton.' Francis stared expressionlessly at the crisp ridge of hair. 'We were talking about sculpture. For the magazine.'

Middleton thrust out his chin. 'Just watch yourselves, that's all. Just watch yourselves.'

Francis, suppressing the urge to curtsey, saw Jamie's head

3

dip beside him as he turned away. 'Philistine,' Jamie whispered.

'Fascist.'

'Hitler.'

'Mrs Hitler.'

Jamie snorted. 'What the hell, though. Look — we've missed the rush hour.' They had reached the cement hub at the centre of the quadrangle; the paths on every side of them were empty. He stepped forward, holding his breath.

Francis smiled and lifted one hand. 'Ciao.'

'Ciao, then.'

As Francis slid into King's Tower he could still hear the metal clips on Jamie's heels, tick-tocking out of the quadrangle. Like stilettos, he had thought in the old days, when their faintest echo had made his heart skitter. A blind whizzed up inside his head and he saw Jamie last winter, spreading a tartan rug on the mud-dotted floor of a boot-room they had never used before. He was surprised it was all so clear; the only light that evening had come from a butterscotch lamp outside the window. 'You look like a sucked sweet,' Jamie had said.

Francis climbed the last few steps of the tower to his dormitory and stretched towards the chipped double doors. They burst violently open towards him.

'Christ! Look out, O'Brien.' Francis flushed, wringing one hand. 'Nearly knocked my fucking arm off. Fucking gorilla.'

O'Brien had changed into the regulation dark blue tracksuit and was massaging his heart. Black hair spurted in the V of the tracksuit top.

'You're really an obscenity, Shagger.' Francis glared into the small, waxy face. The skin was like cheese melting under a grill. 'Really an obscenity. Come and talk to me while I change.'

O'Brien tottered backwards, crashing open the double doors. 'Approach and enter.' He flung out an arm, ushering Francis into the bare dormitory aisle, then leapt to his side and lurched along, hunching one shoulder.

The dormitory was divided every few feet by green wooden

4

walls which stopped short of the ceiling. When they reached Francis' cubicle O'Brien flung himself at the sliding door as if he meant to climb it, and hurled it to one side.

'Sit there.' Francis tapped the lid of a boot-box at the foot of his bed and O'Brien collapsed on to it. 'Just don't piss around. I didn't ask you here to listen to your bollocks.'

'I should hope not.'

'So you can calm down.'

'I'll try.'

'And be sensible for a minute.'

'Sensible, yes.' O'Brien composed his hands neatly in his lap like a child on best behaviour.

'I asked you here because I wanted to hear news about . . .' Francis mouthed 'the bomb factory', then tugged off his shirt and rootled in his chest of drawers. When he straightened again O'Brien was gazing at him uncomprehendingly.

'Bum oratory?'

'You needn't give me any crap, Shagger. If you don't want to tell me, just don't, OK?'

O'Brien pursed his lips. On the crown of his head, his mousy hair was already thin. Silence crackled in the empty cubicles around them.

'Well, don't then.' Francis unbuttoned his flies.

O'Brien made a frenzied rattling at the back of his throat, slid off the boot-box and hopped to the window. Francis turned his back and wriggled naked into his tracksuit trousers.

'These your people?' O'Brien had lounged against the window-sill and was holding a hinged red-leather photograph frame.

Francis sank on to his bed to tie up his gym shoes. 'Yes.' He knew nothing about O'Brien's family. Wasn't his mother dead? 'They're pretty ordinary.'

'No such thing.' O'Brien was vehement.

'What?'

'No such thing as an ordinary family.'

'What, you know about it, do you?'

O'Brien didn't answer but nodded at a picture. 'This your Dad?'

Francis stood up and took the photograph frame, laying it flat on the sill. O'Brien rested a finger on a grey-haired, moustached man outside a flint-covered cottage; he had a colourless drink in one hand and was wearing a beige cardigan with leather buttons up the front.

'No. That's my Auntie Kathleen.'

'Oooh, pardon me,' said O'Brien swoopingly.

'Well, of course it's my Dad, you pillock.'

'Army, isn't he?'

'How do you know?'

'You told me before.'

'Why ask then?'

'I like it, that's all.'

'Tool,' Francis said indulgently, and smiled at the picture. 'He's retired now, anyway.'

'In disgrace?'

'Far from it. He's just old.' Francis hesitated. 'What about yours?'

'Nothing really.' O'Brien was clipped. 'What does he do now, yours?'

'Fuck all. Just sits about saying how busy he is. Gardens a bit I suppose. He has a housekeeper who does most things for him. Cooking and whatnot.'

'Where's the picture?'

'Porlock. We were on holiday. We used to hire a cottage down there sometimes.'

'Oh, I've been there,' said O'Brien, full of enthusiasm. 'Porlock Hill.'

'Yes! It's amazing isn't it? Incredibly steep. Did your car boil over?'

'Not really.' O'Brien paused, colouring slightly. 'We were in a coach.'

Francis spoke without thinking. 'What, a trippers' coach?'

'Yes, that's right,' O'Brien bridled. 'A trippers' coach. We can't all be like you and hire cottages everywhere we go.'

'I'm sorry,' said Francis, offended. 'I didn't mean it like that.'

O'Brien shrugged and turned back to the photographs. 'And here's your Mum.' He pointed to a woman in a windowseat. Her shirt was tweaked up and knotted above a gash of brown stomach. She was wearing three-quarter-length white trousers.

'You know Adele. Everyone does. She's very . . .'

'You call her Adele?'

'Oh yes.'

'Since when?'

'Ever.'

O'Brien whistled softly. 'Far out.'

'She asked us to.' Francis glanced down into the empty quadrangle. The shadows of small clouds loafed across the grass like the shapes of fish swimming above them. The clock-tower struck a quarter and the single note disappeared without a ripple. 'Come on,' he said, suddenly restless. 'I'm meeting someone. Anyway, you'll see her on Sunday if you're at the ten o'clock.'

'Going out?'

'She wants to show off her new husband.'

'New new?'

'A few months.'

'You seem to be taking it like a man.'

Francis closed the photograph frame absent-mindedly. 'I'm used to it.'

'God. What number is this then?'

'Three.'

O'Brien was impressed. 'Shit. What does he do?'

'Don't know really. Something to do with books.'

'Selling them, you mean?'

'Before that. When they've only just been written. He sort of manages writers.'

'Any money in it?'

'Seems to be. He's stinking rich. He's American.' Francis laughed. 'Better than the last one though. The last one was Scottish. This one's a cricketer.'

'An American cricketer?' O'Brien grimaced.

'I know, it's weird, isn't it. He's one of those Yanks who wants to be really English, you know. Drives a Rover, drinks beer. It's a bit pathetic if you ask me. Still, at least it's cricket, not something else. Darts or something. That's where we're going on Sunday – to watch him play.'

'Lucky old you,' said O'Brien sarcastically.

'Well, I like it,' Francis insisted. 'And anyway, we're meeting Catherine there.'

O'Brien whipped the photograph frame open again, and kissed a red-haired girl standing on a pebble beach. 'Oh, Catherine,' he mumbled.

Francis punched him hard on the shoulder, snatched the frame and wiped away the wet O of the kiss with his sleeve. 'You've soaked it, you pervert.'

'I have not.' O'Brien fingered his shoulder. 'Just paying my respects. I know you like it really.'

'Bollocks.'

'You do. Everybody fancying her and everything.' O'Brien darted to the cubicle door, gripped it with one hand and plunged the other deep into a tracksuit pocket. 'Oh yes,' he said, lisping absurdly. 'Mayne's twin? Rather a temptress I should say. The fair Catherine. Rather a temptress.' He jiggled the hand inside his tracksuit. 'Even the great Keith Ogilvie succumbed I think? Am I right?'

Francis lunged at him, but O'Brien sprang away up the aisle yelling, 'Even the great Keith Ogilvie. Even the great Keith Ogilvie.'

Francis peered into the small mirror above his wash-basin, licked his finger and ran it across his eyebrows, smoothing them. They were darker than the straw-coloured hair on his head, and nowhere near joined in the middle like O'Brien's. He practised the slow smile he would give Keith, gradually tightening and stretching his lips and only parting them reluctantly. He wished his face was thinner and his nose more definite; but it would change, Adele said, it was only puppy fat. He smiled again; he was late and Keith would be wondering where he was.

At the end of the dormitory aisle Francis passed Miss Rhodes' sitting-room. She would have heard O'Brien, of course, but it didn't matter. She wouldn't understand. He had already begun to stick out his tongue when her door eased cautiously open.

'Good afternoon, Matron,' he said to the bodiless grey head, clamping his mouth shut as if he had swallowed a fly. Television voices yattered in the room behind her.

'Oh, it's you, Mayne.' The Scottish accent, which parents found soothing, was far-fetched. Francis made an effort not to imitate it.

'Yes, it's me all right. Just off out – rather late I'm afraid; I got held up.' There were tears shining on Miss Rhodes' cheeks like blips of wax. He frowned at her: 'Is everything OK?'

Miss Rhodes shook her head. 'Oh, it's terrible,' she moaned. Her top lip, muzzy with dark hair, quivered. 'Terrible.'

'What is? What's terrible?'

The door crept wider. 'You'd better come in.'

Francis had no curiosity about the room. He glimpsed a row of neatly folded socks on a white shelf like hamsters in a pet shop, and a fat, fleshy-leaved plant. 'It's there,' she said listlessly, pointing at the television.

Francis saw a man lying on a glistening floor, surrounded by people kneeling. After several seconds he recognized him as Bobby Kennedy. Was this a play? If it was, they'd made a mistake – it wasn't Bobby Kennedy who'd been shot, it was John.

'What's happening?'

'It's poor Bobby,' whispered Miss Rhodes, clasping her hands across her stomach. 'They've shot poor Bobby.'

'Is he dead?' Francis asked, but he could see that he wasn't. Someone looking like a waiter, someone foreign, with short black hair and brown skin, wearing a white coat without a collar, was crouched beside him, cupping Bobby's head in his right hand and staring steadily at the camera. It must be a doctor, Francis realized. What did Americans call them? Paramedics? Bobby was concentrating on something in the distance. How smart he looked! The jacket of his dark suit was still buttoned, and the crisp white cuff of his shirt had emerged as he flung up his right arm. You couldn't see where the bullet had hit him. There wasn't any blood anywhere.

'First one and then the other,' Miss Rhodes was murmuring. 'Both the brothers. Ock, but it's terrible. Terrible.'

'It is. It's terrible. Unbelievable.' Standing there side by side Francis thought they must look like people you saw in High Streets, watching television through shop windows. He walked backwards to the door. 'Will you be all right if I leave you, Matron? I'm late to see someone.' He rubbed his neck. 'I'm sorry. He'll want to know about this.'

Miss Rhodes put one hand to her mouth; she did not turn round. Francis left the door ajar and ran downstairs. At the foot of the tower he stopped and gazed across the playing fields towards the wood at the far end. Bobby Kennedy was dying. Now. People would remember this for ever. It would be like when John had died. He would always remember how he had stood outside King's Tower in the sun, looking over the playing fields. At the farthest end, near the wood, a whistle cheeped. That would be something to do with Smith-Henley; he was mad about football, even in summer. Nearer to, loose patterns of boys clustered round french cricketers. To the right, where the ground sank away into an amphitheatre, was the athletics track. O'Brien would be somewhere down there, among those farcical runners and jumpers.

The red brick of the tower was warm behind him. Would Bobby be dead yet? He ought to have stayed and watched. But he wanted to tell Keith. He was really disastrously late now. Keith would understand when he knew why. Francis remembered a photograph he had once seen. Bobby was standing in a paddock, holding the bridle of a pony with one hand and supporting a child – a little boy – on the pony's back with the other. It must have been very early in the morning because Bobby was still wearing pyjamas – just the trousers. But it must have been very warm, too, for him to have stood there like that with nothing on his top half. The low sun splintered like icicles through a line of trees behind him, lightening the child's head and gleaming through the thick mat of hair on Bobby's chest. That was what he remembered most clearly: how the sun in the hair on Bobby's chest made it look as if he was wearing a deep silver shield. A breastplate.

Francis stepped off the tarmac on to the grass shelving down to the lake. Below him, straddling a stream which fed through an iron grill, was a small copse. Years before, when the lake had been excavated, earth had been heaped up in mounds where the copse now stood, its trees huddling together and disguising the unevenness of the ground.

He scrambled over the first few hummocks and the copse grew darker and wilder. Its careering floor was covered with leaves, except where the sun had penetrated in isolated fingers and beckoned up tufts of pale fern. He sheathed his hand in the soft mitten of his tracksuit pocket and squeezed his cock.

Keith was sitting against a tree-trunk, reading a paperback. He had folded the jacket of his suit beside him, and taken off the collar of his white shirt, exposing the hackle of hair on the back of his neck. He looked up and Francis took him in slowly: the lean olive face, the wide mouth, the thatch of absolutely black hair cut short and badly.

'You bastard,' Keith snarled. 'You made me put out my cigarette.'

'I've got bad news, Keith.'

'And you're bloody late.'

'The bad news is why I'm late.' It was crazy, standing over Keith like this. Francis felt like a messenger in a play – a messenger who had rushed into court with news of a battle.

'Bobby Kennedy's been shot,' he blurted, and knelt down. A brown leaf hopped on to Keith's lap.

'What?'

'I've just seen it on Miss Rhodes' telly. He's just been shot. He was lying on the ground.'

'Dead?'

'No, but as good as.'

Keith pushed his glossy black hair straight back from his forehead, and pressed his hand down on top of his skull. His chestnut eyes widened. 'Jesus,' he sighed, winded. 'But that's unbelievable.'

'Isn't it.' Francis felt important.

Keith took his hand off his head and cupped his chin, frowning. His voice relaxed and deepened. 'Of course it's tragic for the Democrats,' he said thoughtfully. 'They haven't got a hope now. He was their best man by miles.'

'He was wonderful.'

'Their only man, really, you might say.'

'Yes.' Francis was excited, but Keith paid him no attention.

'Unless of course there's a backlash. People might vote Democrat just to prove an assassin can't affect them. That's what would happen here, anyway. But perhaps it's too sentimental for America.' He blinked at Francis as if surprised he was still there. 'What do you think, Frank? I'd have said America was pretty sentimental, wouldn't you?'

Francis sat back on his heels and his cock lolled in the loose dark of his tracksuit. 'I don't know,' he said faintly.

'Well, I mean all that cowboy stuff, you know, sentimentalizing your past.' Keith was staring through the trees as if he could see something cantering towards him. 'But there's still the question of who would replace him, of course.' He suddenly faced Francis. 'Was his wife there?'

'I don't know. I didn't see her.'

'No, well they might keep her away. It can't have been pretty.'

'He looked all right, actually.'

'What do you mean?'

'He looked sort of neat and tidy. His hair was still tidy.'

'His hair?' Keith repeated, smiling out of one side of his wide mouth.

Francis was confused. 'What have I said now?'

'Neat and tidy. His hair.' Keith picked the leaf off his lap and closed it between the pages of his book. Francis glimpsed a torn-off head screaming across the cover. 'Still, I suppose they'll find someone,' Keith added decisively.

'Who?'

'Kennedy's people. Someone will appear.'

'They'll have to.' Francis was struggling to concentrate.

'They will; they always do.' Keith rolled towards Francis as if exhausted, and put down his book, propping his head on his hand. Shreds of sunlight skimmed over his hair and shoulder. 'I'd better do something about it for the magazine, I suppose.'

Francis toppled off his heels and stretched out facing Keith. A leaf scratched the small of his back, where his tracksuit had ridden up. 'Shall I?' he asked quietly.

'No, it's all right,' Keith said. 'I will. I'd better. I was thinking I'd do something about Martin Luther King, so I can easily fit this in too. I can send it to Tariq.'

'I don't know why you bother,' Francis said before he could stop himself. 'I mean, you've sent him so much already, and he never bloody well replies.'

'He's very busy,' Keith said, stung. 'Anyway, I don't expect him to reply. I don't want him to, especially. I just want him to put in a word for me somewhere, that's all.'

'Oh well, I expect he will,' said Francis, and looked down. His cock was prodding a pyramid in his tracksuit trousers.

'It'll be quite good really,' Keith went on. 'The mag – what with our Vietnam poll and everything. Quite a strong issue.'

Francis wavered. 'Keith?'

'Mmmn?'

'I really am sorry I'm late. I came as quick as I could.'

'I know. I understand,' said Keith distractedly.

Francis paused again, then said: 'I'd been talking to O'Brien a bit too, actually, before I saw the telly.' Keith stared at him in silence, his gaze flicking from ears to nose to mouth to eyes to hair. Francis turned on the slow smile he had rehearsed. 'I was trying to find out about the bombs,' he murmured.

Keith frowned. 'Do you think he knows anything?'

'I'm not sure. I think so.'

'But he's such a filthy little wanker.'

'He's all right, really. Anyway, it's just the sort of thing he'd do, isn't it? Blowing things up?'

'Is it?' Keith shrugged, then added dismissively, 'You know him better than I do.'

'Oh, I don't know him well. Hardly at all.'

Keith lifted his right hand and tangled his fingers in the hair on the back of Francis' head, dragging their faces close together. 'You prefer to fraternize with older boys, don't you?' he whispered, his breath bitter with cigarette smoke.

Francis gave a little grunt. 'Shit. I thought you'd never notice.'

Keith smeared his tongue over Francis' lips. 'Not going to leave me for O'Brien, then?'

Francis giggled softly. 'Not today.' He craned backwards. Keith's face was smudged but he could see one ear exactly, with its sharply folded outer rim interrupting his hair.

'Anyway,' Keith said, 'what were you talking to Shagger about?'

'Nothing. Just talking, you know. We were looking at pictures.'

'Filthy pictures?' Keith swam into focus: the prominent, downy cheekbones, the scar like a white hair under one eye. He was doing his best to smirk, but his face was too austere. He just looked insane for a moment.

'Family pictures,' Francis said simply. 'Catherine. Heard from her?'

'About a week ago, I suppose.' Keith glanced away through the trees again. 'You?'

14

'We're not letter-writers really.' Francis paused. 'As you know.'

'I don't know. There's lots I don't know.' Keith chuckled. 'Twins' secrets.'

'Oh come on, all that twins stuff is bollocks – all that mystical stuff. You know that. We're just brother and sister.'

'Bollocks, eh?' Keith wormed on top of Francis, pinning him by the shoulders. 'We'll see.'

'Ouch. You're hurting me.'

'I'm not. I'm hardly touching you.'

'You are. You're hurting.'

Keith slid sideways and sat cross-legged. With his trousers tautened, it was impossible to see whether his cock was hard or not. There was a faint redness in his face – a redness underneath his olive skin, shining through it but not mixing with it. 'Take a picture of me,' he said suddenly, burrowing under his coat and producing a camera.

'Why?'

'I feel like it.'

'You don't look like it,' Francis said. 'You look cross. Do you want to be taken cross?'

'I'm not cross. Here. I'll take one of you.'

'No, it's all right.' Francis snatched the camera away and lifted it to his face. Keith was bathed in cold blue light; he had plaited his fingers behind his head and was jabbing his elbows out sideways. Francis clicked a picture: 'Why've you got this here anyway, this camera?'

'I thought we'd take some pix for the mag.'

'What, here?'

'Yeah, you know. "Sunlight In Leaves." The sort of thing *they* like.' Keith paused. 'Alternatively, we could have "The Editor Before Sex".'

'Who said anything about sex?'

'I did. Come here.' Francis put down the camera and tumbled on to the leaves.

'What will it be today, sir?' Keith's voice was wet against his ear.

'Mmmm.'

'Mmmm? We had mmmm yesterday. Still, if that's what Sir wants.'

Francis wriggled on to his back. It was like lying at the bottom of a river; sunlight blobbing through leaves made the air sway heavily. His cock blundered against the waist-band of his tracksuit, and he strained to watch Keith scoop it clear, then kneel above him, his jaw working silently. He knew the way his cock would feel in Keith's mouth: thin, like a pencil, but at the same time weighty and solid.

Keith suddenly flopped down on the leaves. 'Ssssh.'

'What?'

'Didn't you hear something?' Keith sounded parched.

Francis rolled his head, staring through the skeleton of a leaf. More like a fingerprint than a skeleton, he thought. His ears prickled and stretched. 'No, nothing,' he whispered.

'Ssssh,' hissed Keith again.

Francis wanted to laugh. 'What do you think you heard?'

'I'm not sure. It might have been a bird.'

'Is it a bird, is it a plane?' Francis asked, loud and reckless.

Keith stared into his face without seeing him. A pigeon cooed at an obscure distance. 'I could have sworn . . .' He rubbed his forehead. 'I was positive . . .'

'Well, you're all right,' Francis said.

'What do you mean?'

'You've got your sodding trousers on.'

Keith's face lost its severity. He kissed Francis slowly, pushing his tongue underneath the top lip, searching round the gum. Then he sat up.

'What is this really?' Francis drawled, squirming on his bed of leaves. 'Some sort of tease?'

'Wait a minute.' Keith was pointing the camera at Francis' cock. 'Say tease,' he said.

'Teeease.'

There was a cold click.

'One more.'

'That's unfair.'

'What do you mean?' Keith's shining mouth buckled as he pressed his face against the camera.

'What about you?'

'What do you mean, what about me?' There was another click and Francis closed his eyes again. He saw Bobby Kennedy, and the waiter person in the collarless white coat, staring into the camera. The TV lights gleamed on the wet floor. Respect. Who was it who had been saying something about respect? This was showing no respect, being here with Keith. Bobby might not even be dead yet. They kept people alive for ages on machines these days. For ages after they'd otherwise have died. O'Brien. That's who had said respect. 'Just paying my respects.' He'd been kissing the picture of Catherine. Slobbering over it, really. Catherine was standing on a pebble beach with her arms stretched out; she was complaining that the water was too cold to go in.

The camera clicked for a third time and Francis struggled up on to his elbows. 'Don't,' he said, in a little panic. 'Please. Don't; I don't like it.'

Keith lowered the camera and sat astride Francis, trapping his legs, bringing their faces level and inches apart. Keith was sweating, and one eyebrow had rubbed the wrong way. It looked as though a wiry caterpillar had crawled down his forehead.

'Why not?'

'I just don't like it. I'm sorry.'

'It's only a camera; it's only a machine.'

'I know, but it's like having someone else here. Or like your not being here. I can't explain.'

'Oh well, if you really don't like it . . .' Keith's voice hardened; the flush was fading from his face.

'I've said I'm sorry. I'm sorry.'

'Don't keep saying you're sorry, you berk,' Keith said tartly, and put down the camera.

Francis stretched out his arms and draped them over Keith's shoulders. 'Oh gee, Mr Ogilvie,' he said in a silly

17

American accent. 'I'm saary I'm saary.' He collapsed backwards and dragged Keith down on top of him. Keith's legs kicked and straightened like a swimmer's in a spray of leaves, and Francis rolled on to his side. Behind his back he heard Keith spitting into his palm. It sounded disgusted, almost, or contemptuous. He braced his spine.

'Hurt?' Keith murmured.

'Bit. Be gentle.' Leaves pressed against Francis' mouth; they smelled of rotten bark.

'Better?'

'Getting better.'

'Better now?'

'Yes. Better now.' They sounded so witless. They always did – it seemed stupid when Francis remembered it afterwards, but while it lasted it was what he enjoyed best. He liked to think he was overwhelming Keith.

Keith babbled into his ear. It wasn't much of a noise, but that evening, when Jamie told him about the bomb, Francis smiled to think it might have drowned the noise of the explosion.

'What are you grinning about?' Jamie asked. They were strolling down the covered corridor to supper.

'Nothing.'

'It was a serious boom, you know.'

'You're grinning too.'

'Am I?' Jamie laughed. 'Can't think why you didn't hear it. God knows I was busy and I heard it.'

'Nice busy?'

'Quite,' Jamie said, mutedly.

'Only quite?'

'Fuck off and what about you?'

'Very nice, thanks.'

'Sorry to hear it.'

'You see, you *are* jealous.'

'*Encore* fuck off.' Jamie flared his wide nostrils. 'You missed a treat actually, with the bomb. Ripped a whole wall off that shed by the athletics track.'

18

'Blimey.'

'Blimey indeed. Javelins and discuses and things all over the place. And of course utter panic among the athletes. Everyone flying everywhere. Record times set, I dare say . . .'

'I wonder . . .'

'I wonder too.' Jamie's eyes were gleaming. 'Now they're promising us police, would you believe.' They had reached the top of a short flight of steps down into the dining hall.

'Don't ask me, I haven't a clue,' Francis said quickly, gripping the handrail. 'But it's got to be a scientist, hasn't it? Only a scientist could make a bang like that.'

Adele was late for everything. Francis asked her for nine the following Sunday, but it was half past before he sat on his desk, watching from his study window. A line of cars glittered in the drive, and boys sidled towards them in ones and twos. Parents climbed into the sunlight brushing creases from their clothes.

'Hey, Alex,' said Francis. 'Look at this.'

There was the squeaking thump of a chair twitched against a desk.

'No, really,' Francis said. 'Look.'

'I'm *working*, for fuck's sake.' Alex's voice was muffled. 'And you're panting.'

'I'm not.'

'You bloody are. You haven't seen your mother for a month and you're panting.'

Francis twisted round. Pete Townshend, wearing his white boiler-suit, leapt on the wall behind Alex's black, curly hair. 'It was rage,' Francis said. 'Because what's going on out here is so pathetic. All these tools behaving as if they don't know each other.'

'That's right!' Alex looked up, brushing the hair out of his eyes. Thick-set and burly, he had his coat off, and one sleeve of his white shirt was nipped by a black armband. The shirt was ludicrously dishevelled, but above the rumpled collar his face was intense: narrow blue eyes, skin which had once been pitted by acne and now looked sand-blasted. He flung up a brawny arm and the silver foil they had tacked on to their study walls stirred and crackled. 'What the hell do you expect?' he asked. 'Of course they don't know each other. They're emotionally stunted.'

Francis nodded at Alex's desk. 'Finished?'

'No I have not finished. And now I'm obviously not going to finish until you piss off.' He shoved his essay to one side and began drumming on it with a pencil. 'You know what?' he said. 'You're sitting up there just so you can watch little boys. You're a pervert.'

Francis smiled and said nothing.

'A pervert,' Alex insisted, bulking heavily forward and drumming more loudly.

'Same to you,' Francis said. 'All you want is one of those Bedford vans so you can drive around screwing girls in the back.'

'Like Roger Daltrey!' Alex exploded.

Francis gave a dry laugh. 'Roger Daltrey, my arse. You'll never get beyond playing to gangs of Young Farmers.'

Alex dropped his pencil. 'Now now, pervert,' he said in a sarcastic singsong. 'Don't get bitchy, or I'll think you're jealous.'

'Jealous! Do me a favour.'

'Well, we've got to start somewhere,' Alex said earnestly, his big face reddening. 'It's the same for everyone. You have to start with what you know. Young Farmers are what I know. I can't help it. One day it'll be something else – you'll see. Even the Beatles – think of this – even the Beatles began by sending out demo tapes . . .'

'Calm down, calm down,' said Francis. 'I didn't mean it. I'm sure you will. Just keep sending the tapes out and let me know, eh?' He chuckled. 'Why don't you speed up the process and do something a bit out of the ordinary? Why don't you write songs for boys, for instance? Some groups do.'

Alex sat bolt upright and folded his arms. 'Absolute bollocks. Which, for instance?'

'The Kinks, for instance,' said Francis. 'Why do you think they're called the Kinks?'

'It's a word, isn't it? Kink?'

'Yes, Alex,' Francis said condescendingly. 'It is a word. It means bent. Or: having a bend in it.'

'Speak for yourself.'

'I am.' Francis straightened a finger against the glass. 'There goes little Fox, off to see his Mummy and Daddy. I mean, just look at it. How can you resist that, Alex?'

'Thousands haven't.'

'He likes it.'

Alex picked an orange out of the bowl on his desk and hurled it at Francis; it thudded between his shoulder-blades and the silver foil crackled once more. 'I'm sure your mother would thank me,' Alex said. 'How would she feel if she knew her darling wasn't really waiting for her at all?'

'I am waiting for her. It's just that she's bloody late.' Francis looked at his watch. 'Shit. Twenty to. Perhaps I'd better go and wait outside.'

'God, I wouldn't. You'll feel a complete pill with all those parents around.'

'Even so,' Francis said. 'Will you be here after chapel? She'd love to see you.'

'Not sure. We're practising some time this morning – but I will if I can. Anyway; ciao for now.'

'Ciao.' Francis jerked the study door open and shut over a ridge of carpet, and immediately heard his mother's voice. 'Oh yes, thank you,' she was saying. 'Francis Mayne please. He is expecting me. He's my son.' She seemed to be speaking to someone who might not understand English. Francis smoothed his hair across his forehead, tamped it down behind his ear and stepped out of the tower.

She was talking to Rivers, a furry-cheeked Canadian boy. 'Adele!' Francis called. She was wearing a yellow skirt and coat, and a yellow pillbox hat with a dainty white veil. Her fair hair was swept severely out of sight. Everything about her was immaculate and minute; she looked like a cat dressed up.

'Effie, darling.' Her miaou was seductive, yet matter-of-fact.

'Hallo.' Francis ducked to kiss her and the veil tickled his cheek. Over her shoulder he glimpsed Rivers striding away up the drive, tweaking his head up and down by the fore-lock.

Adele's hands slithered off his shoulders. 'Do I pass?' he asked.

She lifted her veil and pinned it, tightening her green eyes. A fleck of powder quivered in one nostril. 'You've got thinner, darling.'

'I can't have done. Not in a few weeks. Anyway, you always say that. I think I've got fatter.'

'Well,' she pouted, 'I can't see if you don't stand straight.'

Francis slid a hand through the crook of her arm and wheeled her towards the tower. Faces whisked out of study windows; three storeys above his head he heard Keith clearing his throat.

'Perfectly bloody journey, as always,' Adele complained.

'But you're all right? I mean; how are you?'

'How do you think I look?'

Francis smiled and said nothing. They reached the mouth of the covered corridor, and a mob of boys parted to let them through.

'It's always so noticeable,' Adele whispered, 'how well-mannered everyone is here. I suppose it's what we pay for.' She looked at Francis soppily. 'What your father pays for, I should say.'

Francis squeezed her arm. Behind them, the notes of a bell were floating into the quadrangle, tinny and brittle above the palaver of banging doors.

The queue for Communion stretched the whole length of the aisle. Most Sundays Francis waited until it had shrunk almost to nothing before leaving his pew, but Adele led him out when he knew they would have to stand in the open for several minutes. Boys were banked steeply on either side, rustling and creaking. He bowed his head, aligning one of his toe-caps with a thread of cement between the black-and-white floor-tiles. Shadows passed him on their way back from the Communion rail; he recognized Middleton's glittering black brogues, and Jamie must be somewhere – he could hear the pert tapping of his metal heels.

He shuffled forwards. He could distract himself by staring at the reredos. Towering behind the altar, its flickering gold frames made up a monumental strip cartoon; each scene was meant to connect with those around it, but each looked self-contained. What had the birth of Christ got to do with the Flight into Egypt? The people didn't even look the same. Slumped in the stable, Mary was just a blob among the animals; when she was on the road to Egypt, draped against a rock under a curving palm tree, she was lithe and exact. She had sharp little breasts.

Francis gazed at other scenes randomly – Lazarus clambering out of his coffin like a man who had been inspecting a drain; the fishermen clawing at their nets. What had any of them to do with the man flopped in his mother's arms, double size, at the centre? He was skeletally thin. Thin as a rake, Adele would say. His rib-cage was like a shell.

The chaplain stooped along the altar rail and Francis focused on the back of Adele's head. Her hair, bleached a streaky white by the sun, bulged as it vanished under the rim of her hat. On the bare nape of her neck, smudged by a few frail wisps, was a dribble of red. Her stork mark.

Adele dithered when she reached the front of the queue. There was room for her to squeeze in at the rail, but this would mean leaving Francis to begin the next batch. She glanced round helplessly.

'Go on,' he whispered.

Adele clicked across the marble. She was like a child, Francis thought, kneeling there next to the bare brick wall. He studied the creamy gaps on the soles of her little yellow shoes; the way her slim calves sagged away from the bone on her legs. Then he looked again at the reredos. At the foot of the cross Mary was crushed under the weight of Christ's body, even though he was so thin. Her face was pinched with the effort of holding him. Grief, presumably, as well as effort. He thought of Keith: the hackle of black hair on the back of his neck; his soft, relaxed voice; the sour tang of tobacco on his tongue.

The organ started into an anthem and the choir scrabbled to their feet. There was the hiss of paper being smoothed, then silence.

Somewhere close behind him a voice whispered: 'Is that Mayne's sister?'

'Don't think so,' whispered another voice. 'Mother.'

'Mother! Shit.'

The anthem began. Francis glanced round, but no faces were visible in the dark wall of pews. He turned back to the altar. The chaplain had stopped in front of Adele and was wiping the lip of the cup with a white cloth. She dipped her head and he tasted the sweet burst of wine in her mouth.

After the service Francis took Adele's arm again as they walked down the covered corridor.

'Shall I just say hallo to Mr Wrexley, darling, before we go?'

'You could,' Francis said grudgingly. 'What do you want to talk to him about?'

'You, of course.'

'You won't get anything interesting from Rex.' Francis released her as they came into the quadrangle. 'But there are a couple of other people . . .'

'Oh?' Adele wavered. 'We must keep an eye on the clock. I told Joe we'd be with him by half twelve, and it'll take us an hour.'

'So there wouldn't have been time for Rex anyway?'

Adele stuck out her bottom lip. 'There's always time for what must be done,' she said officiously.

Francis peered into her face. 'You've got something on your lip,' he told her. 'Lipstick; it's smudged.'

'Have I?' Adele raised her thin eyebrows. 'Bugger. Thank you, darling.' She was still dabbing at her mouth when they reached the drive. Boys were swarming round the waiting cars, and at the end of the line a black Mini was parked askew, looking as if it had nothing to do with anything else. Keith was lounging against the driver's door, ankles crossed, hands deep in his pockets.

Blood tingled into Francis' cheeks. 'Ah,' he said, levelling his open hand like someone offering something invisible to eat. 'Keith, this is my mother Adele. Adele, this is Keith Ogilvie, who I've told you about.' He hesitated, then added stiffly, 'We work together on the mag. He's my editor.'

'Well, *the* editor, anyway.' Keith slowly pulled his hands out of his pockets, ignoring Francis. 'How do you do? Frank's told me a great deal about you.'

Adele fumbled her handkerchief into the sleeve of her blouse. 'Oh dear. Not all insulting, I hope.'

Francis watched Keith holding his mother's hand, then gradually releasing it. 'How did you know which car to wait by?' he asked.

'You told me.' Keith was still looking at Adele.

'Did I?'

'It wasn't difficult,' Keith said. 'I'd have known it wouldn't be like those others.'

'Effie's told you I can't afford a decent car, has he?' Adele smiled. 'I'm very pleased to meet you. I hope you're making Effie work hard on the magazine.'

'He's very helpful,' said Keith gravely. 'I'm hoping he'll take it over next term.'

'You mean, be the editor?' Adele turned. 'You never told me, darling.'

'No, well, it hasn't really been decided yet.'

'I'm sure there won't be any problems,' said Keith. The thick jet slick of his hair gleamed. There was a minute constellation of blood-spots under his chin where he had scraped himself shaving: '. . . yes, and Catherine,' he was saying. 'It is rather extraordinary, isn't it? We met at a dance.' He chortled. 'I expect Frank's told you we have them now.'

'How very broad-minded.'

'I'd have known she was Frank's twin anywhere. They're so alike – apart from the hair of course.'

'Oh yes, the twins' hair,' said Adele, sighing.

'I suppose two redheads would be a bit much. She's well, I hope?'

Francis looked from Keith's mouth to Adele's as if the question were sliding between them on a string.

'Well, since you ask, she's a bit under the weather.' Adele stared between them at the glinting roof of her Mini.

'Oh?' Francis stepped forward. 'Is she? She hasn't said.'

'It's nothing serious. Worrying about exams, I dare say.'

'She hasn't got exams,' Francis said quickly. 'She's like me.'

'No? Oh, I expect it's something else then. You know girls.'

Keith nodded at Adele, smiling knowledgeably, and she took off her hat – uncurling her arm over the top of her head, gripping the rim and tweaking it backwards like a chef removing the cover from a dish. Her hair, dragged fiercely into a bun, was a tight ball of spun sugar.

'You can ask her yourself in a minute, darling.' Adele opened the car door and flipped her hat into the back seat. 'My husband's collecting Catherine,' she explained to Keith. 'At least, I hope he is. It's a pity we didn't know you might be free or we could all have gone together. You should have mentioned it, Francis.'

'I didn't . . .'

'I oughtn't, really,' Keith said complacently.

'Don't you like cricket? We're going to watch my husband play. In Beaconsfield. It's a sort of fun thing, you know. Not serious.'

'It isn't that, it's just work, you know.'

'I can see you must be a good influence on Effie.'

'I try to be.' Keith put out his hand. 'Well, goodbye Mrs . . .' He discovered, too late, that he didn't know her name.

'Zuckerman.' Adele fingered her hair. 'But call me Adele. Everyone does. Don't they, Effie?'

'They do,' Francis said flatly, and walked round to the passenger door. He eyed Keith over the roof of the Mini. 'See you,' he said curtly.

'Tonight? I've got something to show you.' Keith licked his lips as Adele rustled into the driving seat.

'I'll look forward to it.' Francis slid in beside his mother, and she fiddled into reverse.

'That poor young man,' she said as they leapt off down the drive.

'Why?'

'Having to work on a day like today.'

'He likes it – he doesn't really need to,' Francis said sullenly.

'Clever is he? He looks clever. Tell me about him.'

'His parents are doctors.'

'What, both of them? That's nice. Perhaps you'd like to have him to stay in the holidays? I expect he'd enjoy London.'

'He lives there. In Wandsworth.'

'Wandsworth?' Adele exclaimed.

Francis laughed. 'God, you're a snob. I suppose you think that makes them frightfully suburban. Well they're not. They're very interesting. He does something in politics, local councillor, or something. And she writes books.'

'But I thought you said she was a doctor,' Adele said vaguely.

'She is. She writes about doctoring. The National Health, that sort of thing.'

Adele had stopped listening. 'I get you,' she said. 'How very interesting. Sounds very . . .' She let the sentence trail off, and Francis twisted round to see if Keith was still there. Alex was pounding down the drive after them, huge and higgledy-piggledy, like a bullock.

'Oh!' Francis tapped Adele's arm.

'What is it?' She slowed down, looking in her mirror.

'It's Alex Roberts. I thought you'd like to say hallo to him too.'

'Alex? Is he that rather strange boy, the one with the nancy voice?'

'No, that's Jamie. You know Alex. Alex who I share my study with. Enormous Alex.'

'Oh yes, Alex. The one with the skin.' Adele glanced at her watch. 'We are rather late, darling. Will he mind awfully?'

'I don't expect so. He just wanted to see you.' Francis wound down the window as Adele accelerated and shouted: 'We're late!'

Alex billowed to a halt and waved, thrashing one arm violently to and fro above his head.

'I'm sorry, darling.'

'It doesn't matter.' Francis wound up his window.

'Did I see he was wearing a black armband?'

'Yes.'

'Oh dear,' she said spryly. 'Has he lost someone?'

'No. Not really.'

'What do you mean?'

'It's just that a group he likes, The Who . . .'

'Ah, yes. The Who.' Adele congratulated herself. 'I know them.'

'Yes, well, their last single, "Dogs", was a disaster, he thought. So he's wearing a black armband. He thinks they've lost their integrity.'

'When will he take it off?' Adele asked impassively.

'When they get it back again, I suppose.'

'Their integrity?'

'Yes.'

'I see.' Adele's face was blank as they turned out of the drive into the main road. Francis couldn't tell whether she had understood anything he had said.

To reach Beaconsfield they ran along the Thames valley before turning east at Oxford. Everything looked shaggy and prolific – a clump of elms at a junction dwarfed the shimmering traffic; the uncut hedgerows foamed into the road. Climbing the Chilterns in a tunnel of beech, light splashed through the windscreen like flecks of foam.

Adele was preoccupied. Did it have something to do with Catherine? When Francis said: 'So tell me more about my other half,' she answered, 'There's nothing more to say.

She's just a bit low, that's all.' Perhaps it really was all. Perhaps the trouble was Joe? How was their house, he asked. 'Wonderful, darling. It's wonderful being in Chelsea after beastly Scotland.' How were Joe's friends? 'Marvellous. Mainly writers, of course, so all very fascinating.' She seemed happiest to let the lush miles float by in silence. Perhaps she was contented, not preoccupied. Francis couldn't tell; he had never known his mother happy.

When they reached the cricket ground Adele concentrated again. 'I forgot to tell you, darling. Joe's had to bring one of his writers with him.' The Mini pounced to a halt.

'Oh?'

'Yes, he sort of needs help or something, but it's all right. You and Catherine can just buzz off and amuse yourselves, can't you? Now. Where are we?' Adele's head lifted like a dog casting for scent, scanning the rows of cars, the cricketers speckling the pitch, the pavilion. Joe, his legs cased in a pair of huge, yellowing pads, was folded into a deckchair in front of the pavilion. Next to him, but hunched over a drink, was a lanky man with chaotic grey hair.

'Aaah.' Adele patted Francis on the knee. 'Just come and say hallo.' They clambered out of the car and Adele made a tottering run to the back of Joe's deckchair, put her hands on his shoulders and kissed him upside down.

'Oh hi!' Joe sounded astonished. 'Hi, darling! Hi, Frank!' He wrestled himself to his feet and swept a red cap off his head. Long dark curls sprang loose. 'Hi!' He pumped Francis by the hand. 'Good to see you. I got your sis! No trouble, I got her! She's somewhere around, getting an ice-cream, I think.' He draped one arm round Adele. 'Oh, wait a minute, Frank. Just before you go. And Adele, honey. I just want you to say hallo here. Bob.' He beamed at the grey-haired man beside him. 'Bob, this is Adele, and this is my son-in-law, no wait, what are you, Frank, my stepson – this is my stepson Frank. Robert Hales.'

'Oh yes,' said Francis, blushing deeply. Robert Hales. Why hadn't Adele told him? Keith would be beside himself.

Adele extended her tiny porcelain hand but Hales went on staring intently across the pitch. The lenses of his glasses were cloudy with fingerprints.

'Great,' said Joe, shifting from foot to foot like a nervous snowman. 'Bob's over here for a few weeks sorting out some things, aren't you, Bob? That's great. Well, Frank, why don't you just find Catherine. She's getting an ice-cream, or did I say that already? She's by the kiosk there I guess. By the score-box.'

'I'll see you for lunch, shall I, darling?' Adele's voice suddenly tautened. 'What time do you think, Joe? One? Half-past?'

'Don't worry,' said Francis. 'We'll be back. Goodbye for now, Mr Hales.' When he turned away Joe was clattering a deckchair. 'Now you sit here, honey,' he was urging. 'Absolutely here, I insist. It's no problem.' He sounded as though he wanted to sell it.

The cricket ground was divided from the road by a high wooden fence. This had recently been creosoted, and as Francis jinked between the cars the sour air made his face smart. He stopped to blow his nose, bowing into his handkerchief and closing his eyes. Everything around him was sharply developed inside his head: the Union Jack above the white pavilion, the green oblongs on the pitch, the tubby man in the black cap who had just struck away a ball through the slips. Everything seemed separate from everything else, like in the reredos. He stuffed his handkerchief back into his pocket, tilted back his head and stared into the deep blue.

'Funny way to sunbathe.' Catherine's ironical voice came out of nowhere. She was wearing a simple lilac blouse and pleated black skirt; her hair framed her face in burning scoops.

'Christ, Cath, what have you done?' Francis blurted.

She folded her arms and glared. 'Oh, thanks. That's my greeting is it? Thanks a lot. You really know how to win a girl's heart.' She whisked away through a row of cars, the backs of her knees blinking at him.

Francis caught her and kissed the side of her face; she smelt of vanilla. 'I mean your hair, that's all. You didn't tell me. You look so . . . so different . . .'

'It was going to be a surprise.' She stared straight ahead as they hurried past the scorebox, with its two intent faces in their little windows.

'It's very nice,' Francis said energetically. 'It suits you. It looks like Mary Quant.'

'Nice try, but she's got black hair.'

'No, but you know what I mean,' Francis persevered. 'Same shape. It makes you look older. Like Adele.'

'Oh, better and better! Older. Like Adele.' Catherine quickened her pace. When they reached the far side of the pitch she spoke with her back to him. 'I'm not sure I'm going to talk to you. But if I am, it might as well be where no one can listen.'

Francis understood her anger had faded. He gestured towards the few figures scattered round them on the grass. 'Don't you think you ought to announce your highly infectious disease, and clear us a bigger space?'

Catherine sank on to her heels. The black skirt rode up her thighs, and her hundreds of tiny pale red hairs looked like cracks in glaze. 'Give me your coat to sit on, you creep.'

Francis did as she asked and sat beside her. They watched the fielders changing ends.

'Keith sends his love.'

'Oh, Keith,' Catherine said vaguely.

'What about "Oh, Keith"?'

'Nothing. Just: "Oh, Keith".'

'Had a row, have you?'

'He's your friend,' Catherine flushed, 'not mine.'

'He's yours too. It's you that gets the letters.'

'So what?'

'So let's not talk about him if it's going to be like this.' Francis threw a handful of dry grass-clippings into the air. 'I was only asking.'

'You started it. Anyway, it's not like this. It's not like

anything.' She shook her head, then went on neutrally. 'You sound busy, both of you, from what he says.'

'Well, you know.' Francis glimpsed Keith in his study on the top floor of King's Tower, the breeze fingering paper covered with his energetic italic.

For the first time Catherine turned to look at him, and Francis saw how changed she was: the skin stretched waxily over her cheekbones; her freckles like rust. 'But he'll be all right, Keith, won't he?' she said. 'When he goes, I mean. And then you'll be all alone.'

'Not really alone,' Francis was impatient. 'We're bound to stay in touch. We're going to the same college . . .'

'If you both get in.'

'If we get in, yes. And till then there'll be Alex. And Jamie. Masses of people.'

'Not quite the same, though, is it? The rock star and the woofter. Not quite the same sort of . . .' Catherine havered, choosing her words slowly. 'Not quite the same sort of brow level.'

Francis took a deep breath, but decided to say nothing. Catherine was looking across the pitch to the man in the black cap, who had shouted 'One!' and was sprinting out of his crease. 'Keith told me you'd had some explosions,' she said suddenly.

Francis was off guard. 'Yes,' he said.

A single hair had glued itself to the corner of Catherine's mouth. It looked painfully red, tightening like a scar when she spoke. 'Keith says it's all a bit pathetic. He says they've only blown up silly things. What was the last one, a bike shed?'

'The athletics hut, actually. But they're real bombs.'

'He says it's all rather childish and hasn't got anything to do with what's going on.'

'What do you mean?' Francis asked.

'Real demos and things. Paris. Students.' She rubbed the grass in front of her as though ruffling a crew-cut.

'He hasn't said so to me.'

'If you're going to the trouble of making bombs at all, why don't you blow up something worthwhile?'

'It isn't me,' Francis said huffily. 'I don't know what you mean by "you". What do you think they ought to blow up?'

'Oh, I don't know.' Catherine hooked the hair out of the side of her mouth. 'I'm only saying what Keith says.'

'But he doesn't . . .' Francis paused, then said sneeringly, 'specify?'

'Don't be cross.'

'I'm not cross. It's just that he hadn't said any of this to me.'

'Well, let's think of something ourselves then,' said Catherine. 'To blow up, I mean.' She giggled, then suddenly bowed her head. Francis saw the bony silhouette of her bra.

'You OK?'

'Got a hanky?' The hard point of her shoulder jabbed into his chest. 'Sorry. I must have got something in my throat. Grass or something.'

Francis swallowed. 'Adele says you haven't been well. You didn't say.'

'Poor old you. "Nobody tells me anything."' She patted his hand and collected herself, then went on brightly. 'I survived being driven by Joe this morning, that's the main thing.'

'Bad, was it?' Francis asked reluctantly.

'Bad? Miles worse than bad. You know – keeping your inside wheels against the kerb. Shying at corners. Wandering ahead of lorries, then getting into second.' The blue deepened in Catherine's eyes; they glittered.

'Sounds like Granny.'

'It was!' Catherine beamed. 'It was even worse because of that poet. Did you meet him?'

'Robert Hales? Yes. He's incredibly famous – he's a complete hero of Keith's.'

'I couldn't care. He's deranged. Absolutely barking. I couldn't stop him talking in the car. He sat in the back seat – well sort of sprawling into the front – talking about place names the whole time. He told some long story about a place called Malta outside Thame. I couldn't follow it. And bored on about how much more interesting American place names were than English ones. And did I know any streets named after writers.'

'Keith thinks he's practically God.'

Catherine opened her mouth to answer, but a howl from the pitch and a burst of clapping stopped her.

'Jolly good.' Francis knelt up.

'What's that?'

'He's out.' Francis leant his arm on her shoulder and pointed. 'That one there with the black cap, walking away.'

'Oh no, look what's coming,' Catherine moaned. Joe was striding from the apron of shadow in front of the pavilion, with Adele fluttering beside him like a canary. 'I don't think I can bear to look. Poor Mother – how em*barr*assing.'

'It might not be. We know what happens next. It's always the same – he gets a six, or he gets out. It has to be.'

'Why's Joe got on a red cap if the man going out had got on a black one?'

'Because they're not a real team, the Gentlemen of Berkshire. They just get together whenever they can.'

'Is that what they're called? The Gentlemen of Berkshire? But that's ridiculous. I mean it's ridiculous, in this day and age. Anyway, Joe isn't even a gentleman. He's an American.'

'Cath, for Christ's sake.'

She gave a shout of laughter and Francis put his arms round her; her bones felt like papier mâché. 'You are a re-actionary pig,' he said thoughtfully. 'A thin, reactionary pig.'

Catherine snuggled against him. In the centre of the pitch Joe called out 'Middle and leg', in the bored voice of someone ordering a meal they didn't want. A few fielders shuffled backwards and forwards, and the bowler rubbed the ball against a bacon-coloured streak in his crotch.

'Here we go,' whispered Francis. 'Six or out. Bet you.' The bowler pranced into the air and Joe took a large step side-ways.

'A six,' Francis said evenly. 'Baseball; I'd forgotten.'

There was a wet thwack and the ball rose lazily through the wide sky, hovered for several seconds at the climax of its arc, then cracked smartly into the creosote fence. Adele hopped up and down in front of the pavilion with one hand over her mouth. Hales shambled to his feet like a dog roused from sleep; he punched the air and a heavy hank of liquid glinted out of his glass. Adele squealed. There was some laughter and an ancient sodden bellow: 'Shot!'

'What did I tell you?' asked Francis. 'Now – question is: can he do it again?'

An irritated voice crackled above their heads. 'Not if he's got any sense, he won't. Bloody slog. Last over before lunch. If he's got any sense he'll play safe and stay put.'

The voice moved away. 'That was your conscience speaking,' Francis murmured into Catherine's ear. They huddled together and watched Joe meet the next three deliveries with a slouching lean. Then the pitch quickly emptied, to more applause.

Francis released Catherine; the colour had soaked out of her face again. 'Shall we eat, or . . .?'

'OK then.' She quickly dragged herself to her feet and straightened the pleats in her skirt.

'What's the matter?' he asked.

'Nothing. Does it look as though anything's the matter? I'm sorting out this silly skirt.'

Francis slung his coat over his shoulder. 'Don't be upset. We'll stay here if you want.'

'I'm not upset. *You're* upset. You're cross.'

'Don't be silly. Of course I'm not.'

'You are. You're cross with me.'

Francis lowered his voice. 'I told you. I'm not cross. There's nothing to be cross about. I just don't know what you want to do, that's all. Go or stay.' He glanced across to the pavilion where white figures were ambling in its shadows like ghosts greeting each other. Then he put his arms round Catherine's shoulders, leaning his forehead against her, enclosing her. 'Come on,' he said urgently. 'It's me. Me.' His coat slithered on to the grass.

36

She pushed away wearily. 'It's nothing you don't know.'

'But I don't know. I don't know anything.'

'No, well there's nothing *to* know.' Catherine stooped and picked up the coat, bashing grass-clippings off an empty sleeve. 'And as soon as I've had my tests, that'll be that.'

Francis gripped her shoulders again. 'What sort of tests?' He felt he was holding her down; if he took away his hands she might float into the air like a balloon.

'You know. Tests.'

'I don't know. I keep telling you. Where will they be, these tests?'

Catherine wriggled a finger through the hook in his coat; it hung between them exhaustedly. 'Hospital. Because of X-rays.'

'X-rays? What of?'

'I don't know. Head. Chest. That sort of thing.'

'I see.' Francis wanted to lie down. He couldn't concentrate on what she was saying. 'Does Adele know – about the tests, I mean?'

'They told her. And Father.'

'She never told me.' He glanced to the pavilion again. The ghosts had all settled.

'No, well. I never told you, either. Anyway, you know Mother.'

'I certainly do. Here; let me.' Francis took his coat; he was breathing hard. 'But why not tell me?'

Catherine suddenly relented, and stepped backwards smiling. 'Well, I've been feeling all right, really. No temperature. Not in bed or anything. Just fagged out.'

'No headaches or anything?'

'No headaches, doctor, no.' She grinned and tapped his arm. 'Now, let's stop talking about it, shall we?'

'I still can't believe Adele didn't tell me,' Francis said wonderingly. 'She just said you'd been feeling low, that was all.'

'Well, that *is* all. Don't be angry with her. She was probably just trying to help.'

'Help?' Francis exclaimed. 'How?'

'By not making a fuss.' Catherine turned, and they walked slowly on. The red scoops of her hair slithered round her face, shielding her. 'There's no need to make a fuss,' she said gently. 'If there were I'd be in the hospital already. It's just to be on the safe side.'

Francis watched his shoes pressing down the grass, leaving it silver before the blades straightened again.

'No, but I think you . . .'

Catherine interrupted him, hissing, 'Look out; look out,' then saying loudly, 'Oh Mr Hales, I'm so sorry. Have you been sent to find us?'

Hales was swaying by the boundary rope. He had a boiled egg in one hand and a wine glass in the other. 'Your folks . . .' he mumbled.

'We're just coming,' said Catherine.

They moved either side of him and Francis cleared his throat. 'I was very sorry about Bobby Kennedy, sir,' he said ponderously. 'Very sorry indeed. It was a terrible thing.' Hales twitched off his glasses; his eyes were swimming. Francis heard himself go on: 'I mean he was the Democrats' best man really, wasn't he? Who else have they got?' He clenched his fists. When Keith had said that, it had sounded all right. He blinked, and saw Bobby with the sun fuzzing the hair on his chest.

Hales fidgeted his glasses on, and shook his head slowly at Francis. They walked the rest of the way to the pavilion in silence.

When Joe was caught, soon after lunch, the Gentlemen of Berkshire declared and went out to field. Adele coiled in a deckchair, calling to Francis and Catherine to explain what was happening. They talked about nothing, and at tea Francis said he ought to be getting back; he had work to do.

When he straightened from kissing Catherine her smile was fierce, excluding him.

Adele was silent in the car, and as they whizzed across the

Chilterns the light splashing on their knees was worn and tawdry. The evening's first clouds, rolling in from Wales over the Oxfordshire plain, broke the sun into dusty spars and pipes. The sky looked like an attic that had fallen in.

'Shall we listen to *The Top Twenty*?' Adele twiddled the radio.

'It's not on yet,' Francis said drearily.

'I just don't want you to be bored.'

'I'm not bored.'

'I know,' Adele sounded enthusiastic, 'it's ghastly going back. I always used to loathe it. The terrible, terrible sinking feeling.'

'It isn't that. I was thinking about Catherine.'

'What about her?' Adele's lips were jostling minutely together. 'I thought she was fine, didn't you? In good form.'

Francis kept his voice level. 'She told me about the tests and going in to hospital.'

'Oh yes,' Adele chirruped. 'I'd told you about that, hadn't I?'

'No you hadn't, actually.'

'Hadn't I?' Adele was staring straight ahead. 'I'm sorry, darling. I meant to. But it's only a few tests, I expect she told you all about it.'

'She did,' Francis said, his voice still drab.

'She's not worried, is she? She needn't. There's nothing to worry about.' Adele smiled. 'Fabulous haircut, didn't you think?'

Francis gripped his hands between his knees.

'Are you all right yourself, darling? You seem a bit subdued.'

'I'm fine.'

'There are always bugs going round,' Adele rattled on. 'One person gets it, then everyone gets it.'

'Yes.'

'Poor darling. You sound tired. Can you have an early night?'

'I can try.' Once again Francis saw Keith sitting under his

window in King's Tower. He saw the polished brown strap of his watch; the dark soft hair on his arms. 'I've got a meeting about the magazine which may drag on a bit.'

'With that boy we met?'

'Keith, yes.'

'I hope you'll ask him to stay in the holidays. He seemed very nice. Wouldn't he like to come to London?'

'I told you. He lives in London. Wandsworth.'

'Oh, that's right,' Adele said distractedly. 'You did say, didn't you. Doctors. Well, he can just pop across the river, then.' She veered out to overtake a car pulling a caravan, decided against it, and lurched back again. 'Darling?'

Francis said nothing.

'Have you spoken to Dad about the holidays? Only, Joe and I are going to Greece for a bit in the middle, you know, sort of Augustish.'

'I haven't, no.' A dry-stone wall, studded with green and yellow moss, leapt up beside Francis.

'So if you wanted to come late, we could have Keith over then. Or early, of course.' Adele frowned. 'London's always hell in the summer, but still. See how you feel.'

The wall frisked out of sight and a few big fields flapped like tablecloths. If Adele said anything else before they turned into the drive, Francis didn't hear it.

The shadow of the tower fell across them. 'You know you can ring me at home at any time, don't you?' Adele put her warm hand on his knee.

Francis flinched. 'I'm sorry Joe didn't make it into double figures,' he said.

'I thought he did jolly well. I'm sorry we forgot your sweets, darling.'

'Sweets!' Francis exclaimed. 'Whatever made you think of sweets? I haven't had sweets for years.'

'It's nice to have something from home.' Adele leant towards him. Over her shoulder he saw faces floating into study windows and closed his eyes, inhaling the dizzy scent of her powder.

Then he struggled out and went round to her window. 'Goodbye, Mrs Zuckerman,' he said.

'Goodbye, Master Mayne.' The car bounded forward as she spoke, hooted twice and accelerated away. Francis watched the indicator light winking at the end of the drive. When it vanished, the evening was immediately darker. On the playing fields, figures were crouching round a slip cradle; he could hear the sound of their voices, but not the words they were saying.

A rasping guffaw broke from a window behind him. The light in his study was out – where was Alex? He crossed the gravel into the bright corridor, shouldered his door over its ridge of carpet, and clicked on his lamp. On his desk-top, dotted with crumbs of fruit cake, were a piece of notepaper and a large brown envelope. The note was from Alex: 'Sorry to miss you this a.m. Back about nine. Rock on!' Francis scrumpled it up, then opened the envelope, using a biro as a paperknife. Inside were photographs, about a dozen of them, and a message from Keith. He fanned the pictures out, blood charging into his face. He saw his cock rearing away from him, desperate to avoid his gaze and meet that other face which was also his – flattened and peering like Gulliver tied down in Lilliput. He saw a pearl of sperm; a leaf skeleton. He saw slack, splayed skin and wiry hair. Then he saw his hands shuffling all these things together and squaring on top of them the note from Keith: 'Thought you'd like to see these. Good for the mag, do you think? I've got the negs, so behave yourself. Come up and see me sometime.'

No one knew anything about the next bomb until a spoon banged on a table at the end of lunch.

The square face at the end of the dining hall was embarrassed. 'Thank you, gentlemen,' it said carefully. 'Today a cloud is over us. We have suffered, as you know, two incidents . . .' There was a snort like tearing cloth, and Francis crouched over the table-top, studying its stains and scratches. 'It's not funny,' he heard. 'Some of you might consider this amusing, but it is not amusing.'

A snake hissed a few places away. That must be O'Brien. Then the voice began again, rising and falling nervously, so Francis only heard it in scraps. 'But I'm not talking . . . I almost wish . . . this morning . . . outrageous one . . . the village sewage . . . ruined.'

Francis tingled as though he'd been slapped. From behind him, where the snort had let rip, came a distraught gasp. He made himself think of Catherine. How ill was she? Her face, china white between the glowing commas of hair, floated through his head. Her hair was like quotation marks. Her hair was quoting her face.

He looked up the hall at the solid body in its long black gown. Ruined. What did the word mean? He risked a glance at Keith; he was heavily slumped, chin in hand, bored. 'It's heinous,' the voice said, speaking more slowly now. It must nearly have reached the end. 'We live in turbulent times, as those of you who read the newspapers appreciate. Turbulent times . . .' The next thing he knew was shuffling to his feet, and the boys rustling as though a breeze was blowing over them.

In the scrum round the door Francis struggled to reach

Keith, but his sleek head vanished. Alex appeared. 'What do you reckon?' he panted.

Francis was suddenly impatient. 'What about?'

'About the bomb, spaz. What else? Isn't it hilarious? Did you hear Jamieson having that fit?' They climbed the half-dozen steps out of the dining hall and crushed along the covered corridor.

'I didn't recognize him,' Francis said carelessly.

'He completely got the giggles.'

'I didn't think he'd got a cold, exactly.'

Alex was insulted. 'What's got into *your* nappy?'

'Nothing. The bombs are a bit silly if you want my opinion.'

'Silly? I think they're hilarious. Think of all that crap flying into the air.'

'I am thinking of it,' said Francis loftily. 'And what I'm thinking is: if you're going to go to the trouble of making bombs you ought to blow up something worthwhile.'

'*Worthwhile?*' Alex sneered. 'We're talking about the village sewage plant here. Isn't that *worthwhile*? You sound like bloody Ogilvie.'

Francis shoved his hands into his pockets. 'Well, that wouldn't be so surprising, would it – I mean, we're friends.'

'Oh come on, fuck off, what's the matter with you?' Alex stood aside to let Francis through into the quadrangle, and shoved him in the small of his back.

'Don't fucking push me around,' Francis snapped.

'I hardly touched you.'

Francis stood still. Alex was hands on hips, lowering. 'Oh, I don't know,' Francis groaned, and shook his head. 'I'm sorry.'

They walked on a few paces in silence, Francis smoothing his fringe. Then Alex said grumpily: 'How did bloody Ogilvie's bloody exams go, anyway?'

'I'm just on my way to find out. The last one was this morning.'

'Bloody brilliant, I suppose.'

'Probably. His others have been OK. What about you – where are you off to?'

Alex brightened. 'Band practice.'

'Always bloody band practice.'

'Piss off.' Alex gripped Francis above the elbow and squeezed.

'Ouch, that hurts, you arsehole. What did you do that for?'

Alex leant close and whispered, 'I wouldn't say arsehole too loudly if I were you, my old arsehole.' His breath smelled of custard.

Francis glanced ahead to the tower and saw Rex rocking on his heels in the doorway. His arms were folded inside his gown as if he were cold.

'Ah. Good afternoon, Roberts. Mayne.' The shy pink face swivelled and blinked under its ebullient bush of brown hair.

'Lovely day, sir,' Alex said chirpily.

Rex ignored him. 'Mayne, I was rather hoping to see you.'

'Me, sir? Absolutely, sir.' Francis pressed open the tall door into the tower. 'I was just going to get changed. I was just going to a meeting.'

Rex said nothing but went on rocking from heel to toe, frowning at the mosaic floor.

Francis' arm began to ache. 'Shall we go then, sir?'

'Shall we?' Rex plunged past Francis down the study corridor, his rubber soles wheezing, his hair bouncing up and down. As Francis followed, he heard Alex mutter, 'He thinks you're the bomber. Better get your alibi ready.'

Rex closed his study door and pointed to one of the ancient leather armchairs by the gas fire. Boys were never invited to sit in these chairs. Fear fizzed up Francis' legs and he looked round erratically. There were the silver cups on the mantelpiece. There was the desk, with its unblemished blotter, and the little bottle of Nippon ant-killer that had been waiting unopened for ever.

Perhaps it wasn't about the bombs at all. Perhaps it was Keith. A blank grey washed the bay window. What had Alex meant, saying it was a lovely day? It was a perfectly ordinary day.

Francis sat down. Rex had sunk deep into the chair opposite and clasped the dumpy brown wings protruding either side of his head. He looks so awkward, Francis thought; he looks as though there's this enormous black woman kneeling behind him and he's holding her tits: no wonder his face is pink; he's blushing.

'I'm sorry it's a touch chilly in here, Francis. Are you chilly? I could turn on the fire.'

Francis stared at the drained honeycomb on the wall between them; at the large yellow box of matches pressed neatly against its metal tap. 'No thank you, sir, I'm fine. But if you . . .'

'No, I'm fine too, thank you. It is June, after all, June.' Rex blew out his lips, then suddenly snatched his hands off the leather tits and crossed the room to his desk. 'I'll come straight to the point.' He turned round, opening and closing an envelope like a small, stiff lung. 'I've had a letter from your father, the brigadier, and I'm afraid it has bad news in it. He's asked me to tell you before you go home. I mean, you'll be going home immediately – there are only a few more days left here anyway. He doesn't want you to go home without knowing.'

Rex tweaked his trousers and crouched into his chair again; the white envelope was sticking up from the hand in his lap. Through the wall came the clatter of a boy running down the study corridor in cricket boots. That was illegal.

'It's about your sister Catherine. I think you know – your father says you know – she was going to have some tests.'

You needn't go on, Francis thought. I know what you're going to say; you can leave me alone now. A cloud shuffled across the glass in one of Rex's pictures. It was the framed poster of a play that had been put on years ago: *The Lady's not for Burning*. The poster was a watercolour and showed a boy standing in front of a fire – a neat, beautiful fire, like the stripes on a shell. But it couldn't be a boy, could it? It must be a girl. A lady. She looked faded by the sun, now that you could see the picture clearly because the cloud was over it.

When the cloud drifted on, the picture dazzled and disappeared again. How many times had Rex had to say things like this before: 'I have some very bad news.' Years seemed to have passed since they had sat down a moment ago.

Francis had pins and needles in his calf, but his leg was too heavy to move. 'What are you saying exactly, sir?'

'The tests show she has leukaemia.' Rex's voice was expressionless.

'I see. And will they let her go home? I mean, what's happening?'

'Your father was collecting her this morning. They think she might be better at home.'

'I see,' said Francis. His brain was a dry walnut. 'That means she's very ill, doesn't it?'

'They're doing everything they can, but your father says the hospital would prefer that she were at home, for her sake. With her family . . .'

'My mother isn't there,' Francis said irritably. 'I mean, she's not there, and anyway she's about to go away on holiday.'

Rex gave a little cough. 'Your father has other help, doesn't he?'

'Yes, sir. Mrs Banyard. She's been there for years – she's a sort of housekeeper.' The envelope ticked to and fro in Rex's lap, and Francis imagined the brigadier's Daimler swinging up the short drive at home. He saw Catherine lying along the back seat under a tartan rug, her face splotched with shadows from the chestnuts overhead.

'Will she die, sir?'

'I can't answer that,' Rex said evenly. 'She's very ill.'

'Why's it got so bad? Why didn't she have more warning?' Francis wished he wasn't whining.

'I'm afraid I can't answer that either. She's a very brave girl, your sister.'

The words splashed over Francis, soft and difficult to understand. He saw the Daimler stop, and the white front door opening. Out bundled Mrs Banyard, squat, shielding her face at the back window of the car. Catherine's smile flicked like a fish in a dark pool. His father hefted her up in his arms and swung her inside – one arm under her shoulders, one under her knees.

'So what I suggest,' Rex was saying, his voice still level, 'is that you go and see Miss Rhodes immediately about your packing. I'll take you into Oxford for your train early tomorrow. If we leave at eight we should be fine.'

'Thank you, sir. You've been very kind, sir.'

'If there's anything else, Francis. Anything at all . . .'

'Thank you, sir.' Francis jumped to his feet. He wanted to leave immediately. This had nothing to do with anyone else. He wanted to be alone. Clearly something important was happening, something which was not his fault. It marked him out.

'See you at eight then, sir.'

'Remember; anything at all.' Rex was silhouetted against the bay window; his bush of hair looked like a cartoon; his long arms dangled limply.

Francis shoved into the corridor and saw Alex ducking into their study. 'Hey. Arsehole,' he shouted. 'Wait for me.'

The top floor of the music school was divided into practice rooms, with a large rehearsal hall at one end. Francis climbed the metal stairs past a dribble of piano music and the sour parp of a trumpet.

O'Brien shimmied towards him. 'Jesus, Mayne. I'm incredibly sorry. Really incredibly.'

Francis was confused. 'Shagger! What are you doing here?'

'Just listening. Alex Roberts asked me – I'm the roadie.' O'Brien's face was pinched, as if it had been squeezed by a pair of enormous hands. 'I don't know how to say it,' he went on. 'I'm just incredibly sorry.'

Francis took pity on him. 'It's all right,' he said gently. 'Alex told you, did he?'

'He did. He told us all – all the band. He said you might

be coming over when you'd packed and everything, but we didn't expect you. I mean . . .' O'Brien faltered, clenching his fists.

'Is everyone there?' Francis glanced over O'Brien's shoulder towards the practice hall. 'The whole band?'

'Yes.' O'Brien pressed to one side of the corridor.

'Well . . .' Francis smiled wearily. 'I didn't want just to sit in my study, you know.'

He stepped round O'Brien and pushed open a pair of double doors. Alex immediately bounded forwards running his meaty hands through his hair. 'You're here! Amazing!'

Francis nodded heavily. Eyes were staring at him, and he couldn't think clearly. He couldn't remember why he wanted to be there.

'You know everybody.' Alex swung round like a host at a party, pointing towards a dais under a tall window, and Francis saw three boys who had taken off their coats and ties. One of them had a multi-coloured scarf knotted round his throat. 'Hey,' they called. 'We're really sorry. We are. We're really sorry.'

Francis edged away, but Alex was gripping him by the arm. 'It's great to see you,' he said breathlessly. 'What do you want to do? Sit and listen for a bit? Or aren't you going to stay? Why don't you sit at the back there with Shagger?' He bowed close; a trickle of sweat had dried in a slug-trail down one cheek. 'It's pathetic about Shagger. He wants to be our roadie – but, I mean, we never go on the road. Never mind. He's timing our songs. It'll help with the tapes.'

'Oh yes, the tapes,' Francis echoed.

Alex frowned. 'You sure you're OK?'

Francis gazed into the big, pitted face. 'I'm fine,' he murmured. 'Fine. I'm just a bit . . . you know, a bit tired.'

'Of course you are,' said Alex, releasing him. 'You're bound to be. Why don't you go and sit by Shagger, then. It's a good idea.'

Francis veered away through a clump of music-stands and sank down at a long table.

'Hi!' O'Brien was enthusiastic, as if greeting him after a long absence.

Francis couldn't think what to say. He watched Alex lurch on to the dais and heard him boom through the microphone: 'Hey! Frankie! We're going to do one of your songs, OK?'

'Great!' shouted O'Brien, and pulled a notepad out of his pocket.

'Just time the fucking thing, you, and stop talking,' came a cold voice.

Francis forced himself to speak. 'What's eating Savoury?'

'Nothing special. Just being himself – you know what he's like.' O'Brien jiggled a leg nervously under the table. 'Hang on. Here we go.'

Alex gripped the microphone with one hand and jabbed the other above his head. Francis saw Robert Hales jumping out of his chair at the cricket match, punching the air. Drink sloshed on to the grass and Catherine's hair tickled his face. Then she was in their father's arms, whisked into the dark hall at home.

'Great song!' O'Brien's voice was warm against his ear. The music staggered as Savoury missed a beat, but crashed on. It was like talking in a cave behind a waterfall; they were shouting but private.

'I loathe it.'

'What?'

'I said I loathe this song,' Francis mouthed.

O'Brien slid the notepad in front of him and tapped it. 'Write another one then.'

'Don't be a moron.'

O'Brien rolled his eyes.

'You're not timing them. What's the matter with you?'

'No pencil.' O'Brien clawed out the contents of his pocket, spreading everything on the table. 'Know what this is?' His hand closed and opened again in Francis' lap, almost touching his trousers. In his palm was a bottle-top with a jagged hole in it, and a piece of waxed string poked through the hole.

'Yes,' said Francis dreamily. 'It's a timer.'

'I knew you knew,' O'Brien beamed. 'I told Gower you did.'

'Gower?'

'You know,' said O'Brien. 'Gower. Who does the bombs with me.' He paused. 'You looked round at us that day in chapel when your mum was here, when you were going up for Communion. You looked right at us.'

'Shagger, I couldn't see you when I turned round,' Francis said sorrowfully. 'I heard voices, but all I could see were the pews. It was too dark.'

'Oh bollocks.' O'Brien blanched.

'For God's sake, it doesn't matter.' Francis brightened. 'I'm not going to tell anyone. Anyway, I'm going away tomorrow.' He nudged O'Brien's shoulder. 'I had a pretty good idea, of course.'

O'Brien grinned again; one of his front teeth was chipped. 'I knew you did. I just knew it. I said so to Gower.'

The song ended and O'Brien swept the odds and ends off the table back into his pocket. 'Great,' he called. 'Three minutes twenty-eight seconds. Your man here's just writing you another one. Ready in a minute. Just play something else and it'll be finished.'

'It fucking well won't be,' Francis said, but his words were drowned as the band set off again.

O'Brien was holding up a grimy stub.

'Call that a pencil?' Francis twisted it out of O'Brien's hand, pulled the notepad towards him, and wrote without thinking:

> Oh when my baby left me
> It made me sad and blue,
> It made me feel like I'd been hit
> With Sister Limm's hot spoon,
> Oh yeah, with Sister Limm's hot spoon.
>
> So I lay me down in the greenwood
> And stared right up at the sky

And I thought that a hole between the clouds
Was the place I'd go when I died,
Oh yeah, the place I'd go when I died.

Then I heard the grass a rustlin'
Right under the greenwood trees,
And I turned my head around to look –
Hallo sweetheart or hallo the breeze,
Oh yeah, hallo sweetheart or hallo the breeze.

Well, what do you think I saw there,
It's true, so help me God,
A twitchin' right out of the trees was not
My baby but Mister Tod,
Oh yeah, not my baby but Mister Tod.

So I knew for sure I'd lost her,
I'd lost my sun and moon,
My day and night all shot to hell
By Sister Limm's hot spoon,
Oh yeah, by Sister Limm's hot spoon

O'Brien's laughter was shaking the table. 'Bloody hell,' he
wheezed. 'How do you do it? Not that I can understand a
word.'

'Yes you can,' Francis told him. 'You know about Sister
Limm's hot spoon.'

'Everyone knows about that. I mean, all this stuff about
the greenwood tree.'

'Oh, that. That's nothing. When I was in the wood by the
lake, once, I saw a fox – that's all. It just came up to me,
really close, then went away.' Francis leant forwards, reading
through what he had written. Tears splashed on to the
notepad, and he realized they must be falling from his own
eyes.

'What a weird thing to do.' Keith was cross-legged on the
red cushions in the alcove of his study at the top of King's
Tower. His desk-lamp was the only light, poised against the

deep black of the uncurtained window. 'What on earth did you want to see all that lot for?'

Francis was abashed. 'I didn't know it was going to be all that lot. I thought it would just be Alex.'

'But it's a *band*, Frank. Of course they'd all be there.'

'I know it's a band. I wasn't thinking. I didn't know what I was doing. I just wanted to see someone. I'd looked for you, but you were out.'

'Library,' said Keith crisply, then sighed. 'Anyway, what did you do after you'd left them?'

'Oh, you know. Hung around. Eventually I went back to my room and read a bit.'

Keith relented a little. 'Anything good?'

Francis stared from his wicker chair at the poster facing him. Naked pixie figures cavorted in a silver mist, and beneath them it said: The Soft Machine Turns You On. His head flopped sideways. 'Can't remember, really.'

Keith reached down and rubbed Francis' ear with a long olive finger, as if he were stroking a cat. 'Tired?'

'You're the one who ought to be tired. But yes, I am tired. Ever since I saw Rex I've been fagged out. It's peculiar.'

Keith lounged back in the alcove; it was lined with a dark-green paisley shawl. 'It's a perfectly natural reaction, feeling tired. A perfectly natural reaction to stress. But you needn't worry about the mag when you go. I'll do all that. I'm pretty sure Rex has decided about you taking over.'

'Jesus,' Francis sighed hopelessly. 'I can't even think about tomorrow, let alone anything further off. I don't feel I'll be anywhere tomorrow. After tonight I probably won't exist.'

'Come on, Frank,' said Keith firmly. 'Don't let it get to you like that. Here's where you'll be. Not tomorrow, but after the summer. Like me. There's nothing any of us can do.'

'We can look after her.'

'I meant that of course. I just meant we mustn't be sentimental.'

'We?'

'I'll be thinking of you, of course,' Keith said importantly. 'Both of you.'

'Keith?' Francis narrowed one eye and a paw of wind stroked the window, rattling it. 'There is one thing. What have you done with those photos, the ones in the wood?'

'Don't worry about them.'

'I'm not worried. I just wondered, that's all.'

Keith was obstinate. 'Well, don't.'

Francis licked his lips. 'I'll miss you,' he said thickly.

'I'll miss you too, but you mustn't think about me.'

'I won't be able to help it.'

'You must concentrate on Catherine. Don't think about me. Don't ring me. Don't even write.'

'You can't only have one sort of thing in your life. You have to have another, even when it's like this.' Francis was too tired tired to explain what he felt.

'You're babbling,' Keith told him.

'I must be falling asleep.'

Keith stood up and clicked off the desk-lamp. The silver pixies writhed in the darkness.

'Why did you do that?'

'What?' Keith pulled a cushion from the alcove, dropped it on the carpet, then knelt and undid Francis' trousers, tweaking the belt-end out through the buckle with an eager flip.

'Turn out the light like that.'

'So you could go to sleep.'

Francis wriggled down in the chair until his head and knees were almost level.

By the middle of August, when Francis had been home nearly two months, Catherine no longer shocked him. The day he arrived, and found her waving at his taxi from the front step, he thought there was nothing wrong: the results of her tests had been muddled with someone else's; she had miraculously got better. He had pulled her face on to his shoulder and kissed her warm hard head.

The brigadier had made up a small room downstairs – the one he sat in during the winter. Its fire basket cowered between heavy plaster columns, and on each was painted a crude coat of arms. Most of Catherine's visitors asked to have them explained. 'They're the arms of the see of Canterbury and the see of Chelmsford,' she would say. 'Canterbury because it's Canterbury; Chelmsford because of where we are. The house used to be a rectory before Dad bought it.'

She pretended to admire the fireplace, but in fact it oppressed her. 'Flowers will not wither it, nor get-well cards blah blah blah,' she had said when she first led Francis into the room.

'You've got yourself well set, anyway.' He had edged round the bed and looked out of the window. A huge chestnut rustled in the field across the drive.

'I'd rather have my own room, but Dad thinks it's less like a bedroom here. He says he'll like to have me near when I'm resting.'

That evening Catherine had fallen asleep by eight. Francis unpacked, then came to find his father watching the news in the sitting-room. The brigadier had turned off the television and closed the doors of the cabinet over its face. With his back to the french windows he told Francis about Catherine's tests. As if commending a brave soldier, he said she had amazed the doctors by being so active when so ill. But it couldn't last more than two or three months. Six at most. Francis must understand that. Catherine herself didn't know – at least, she hadn't been told. There wasn't any point in hospital; there wasn't anything to be done.

The brigadier's voice had been gentle; occasionally he ran one finger along his top lip, brushing his grey moustache. Stiff upper lip, thought Francis; he's stiffening his upper lip. The heavy, florid face was withdrawn and baffled. Only once had he sounded stirred – when he described the disease as 'galloping', and gave a little shrugging buck. Loose change jingled in his pockets.

In the following fortnight Catherine seemed to leak air. She stooped; her clothes bagged on her; her eyes hardened and shrank into their sockets. Francis wished he had never thought about the leak. Every time the district nurse called, or the doctor, he imagined they were scrabbling under her clothes to find the hole. It was farcical. He even had a dream of the doctor kneeling beside her, pressing his face to her stomach, saying: 'If there's the slightest escape I'm bound to feel it against my cheek. It's the surest way.'

After a month she stopped bothering to get dressed. Her bedtime crept forward into the early evening and her afternoon nap extended to meet it. Francis expected that he and his father would be drawn more closely together, but neither of them made the first move. After their evening meal the brigadier sat erect in front of the television, repeatedly clearing his throat with a curt hack, until the news ended and Francis went to read in his room. Mrs Banyard kept to the kitchen. Whenever Francis saw her they never mentioned Catherine.

Francis liked the routine of his days. To wake at the same time; to help make Catherine's bed; to sit with her and occasionally walk arm in arm round the garden; then to draw her curtains and tiptoe away into the hushed house, made him believe he might slow down her illness. It was obvious he couldn't stop the air leaking altogether – hardly a day went by without her seeming smaller. Her hair perched on her scalp like a wig, and when a strand caught in her mouth she no longer noticed. She would continue talking with what looked like wires jerking along her cheek. Francis itched to brush them away, but knew she would resent him. Just as she would resent him if he asked to snip off the tough black hair which had wriggled malevolently out of the mole beside her mouth.

The early morning was her best time. When Francis took in her breakfast tray she would be curled in the broken-looking pink armchair under the window.

'Sleep all right?'

'Like a log.' Her answer was always the same, and she always made a fuss over the tray. 'How yummy. Cereal *and* an egg.'

'Well, Mrs Banyard did it really.'

'Yummy, yummy. *And* my pills.'

She never finished her meal, and at nine the post van would spurt up the drive and distract them. Francis hurried to the front door; it was one of the few times of day he was sure to see his father.

When Adele's card arrived, the brigadier handed it to him with a wedge of other envelopes: 'Writing here I recognize.'

Francis read as he walked back to Catherine's room. At the top Adele had crossed out 'Monday' and scrawled 'Whoops! Tuesday.' It went on: 'Darlings. Isles of Greece fabulous. Just back to find letter from yr father – wonders never cease! Coming down next Wed to take you both out. Desperately worried. Lots and lots of love, Adele. xxx'

Francis propped the post on Catherine's tray. 'Madam has a communication from Desperately Worried of Chelsea, who is coming to see Madam.'

'What?'

'Our mother has written to us.' He sat on the bed, facing Catherine in her chair. 'She's coming to see us.'

'But she can't. It'll mean seeing Dad.'

'Well, he'll have to go out or something.'

'He can't. Why should he? He'll refuse. I know he will.' Catherine was reading the card as she spoke; she sounded appalled. 'We'll have to go out.'

Francis hesitated. 'We'll see. We could.'

'We'll have to.' Catherine shook her head and colour washed into her cheeks. 'Hope she comes alone.'

'You mean Joe? Surely . . .'

'She might bring anybody. A hippy. A lion-tamer.'

'I'd like to see Dad turn away a lion-tamer. "I say, old chap, would you mind awfully . . .?".' Francis imitated the brigadier clearing his throat. 'What else have you got there?'

'Card from school friend. Letter from school friend. Something for you.'

'Oh Christ, it's from Rex.'

'Perhaps you're going to be expelled.' She flipped a long white envelope into his lap and went on listlessly: 'Another card. Another. And this.'

Francis glanced sharply away. 'That's from Keith.'

'I know.'

'Why's he written to you?'

'Why shouldn't he? He often writes to me.'

'Not since you've been home he hasn't.' Francis poked his finger hard into Rex's envelope, ripping it open. The full stops between the initials at the end each had a smudgy tail. Rex would have written it at his desk in the gloomy study. He would have paused and seen the unopened bottle of Nippon. He would have heard the silence outside in the deserted quadrangle. Francis pursed his lips. It was all right. Of course it was all right for Keith to write to Catherine, not to him.

'What's the news?' Catherine asked.

'Oh, it's about the magazine mainly, boring. And Keith's exams. He obviously did amazingly. Does he say?'

'Haven't read it yet. God, it's endless.' Catherine was counting the pages, holding them at arm's length. At the foot of the last sheet Francis saw: 'All my love, Keith.'

'Nothing for you,' she said cheerily. 'Sorry.' She slid the letter back into its envelope.

Francis tried to sound uninterested. 'Aren't you going to read it then?'

'I'll read it later. Why are you blushing?'

'I'm not blushing.'

'You are. You've gone bright red.'

'I haven't.'

'You have. You're as red as a beetroot.' Catherine pointed at him, her eyes glittering. 'You're jealous.'

'Of course I'm not jealous. Why should I be jealous? It's quite right he should write to you. You're the patient.' He glared out of the window. The chestnut's enormous bell skirt was tattered and floppy. A blackbird whirled up inside it like a scrap of charred paper caught in a draught

'Perhaps Keith'll have heard from Tariq Ali at long last,' Francis said flippantly, but there was no answer, and when he turned back to Catherine her eyes were shut.

'Catherine?' He held his breath. She was asleep – her nightdress rasped delicately as it rose and fell against the edge of Keith's envelope. He picked it up, supporting it on his flat palm as if trying to guess its weight. Then he put it down in her lap and left the room. As he closed the door he heard a little strangulated gulp. Catherine had woken up again – or perhaps she had only been pretending to be asleep. The letter gasped as she tugged it out of its envelope.

The brigadier left a good two hours before Adele revved to a halt. Francis opened her door and a sweet blur of scent and cigarette smoke escaped like a genie out of its bottle. She was wearing a loud black-and-white check, and her hair was sculpted round her face. She was deeply tanned.

'My God, darling, have you heard?' she burst out, staring up at him through dark glasses.

'What? You are brown.'

'Czechoslovakia. It's been invaded. The radio's buzzing with it. I've been listening all the way down. That poor Mr

Dubcek.' Adele thumped her lap. 'I knew it couldn't last, and now it's tanks all over the streets. He'll be lucky not to be put against a wall and shot. Those *vile* Russians.' She whisked off her glasses.

Francis saw Keith lounging against the tree by the pond; it was like poor Bobby. Keith would want to know. 'I had no idea,' he said feebly.

She picked a thread off her skirt, rolled it into a ball, and flicked it on to the drive. 'I'm sorry, darling. What a way to greet you.' She climbed out and kissed him, pressing a cold earring against his mouth. 'Tell me everything.'

'Well, I'm . . .'

'Is your father here? Sorry to interrupt.'

Francis slammed the car door. 'No; he had to go out.'

'I don't mind seeing him. You know that.' Adele put her dark glasses back on, and stared at the house: the blinding white walls, the trim bushes either side of the front door, the large inky windows.

'Never changes a bit,' she sighed. 'You're very lucky.'

Francis steered her down the drive.

Adele giggled. 'Where are we going?'

'I don't want Catherine to think we're plotting,' he said severely. 'But you can't possibly go in and see her without knowing what you're doing.' They were already under the chestnuts.

'Don't be ridiculous, of course I know what I'm doing. I'm her mother.'

'I mean,' Francis swallowed, 'before you know how ill she is.'

Adele stopped. 'Oh God,' she gasped, and pulled away from him. Small shadows bobbed across her forehead and one cheek. The other cheek was in bright sun and its crust of powder looked like sugar on a cake. 'Oh God,' she gasped again. 'I can see it in your face.'

Francis glanced at the tarmac and heard his father's voice complaining about the cost of surfacing the whole drive.

'You'll see a great change in her,' he said steadily. 'She's quite cheerful, though. Remarkably cheerful, everyone says.'

Adele was biting her lip. 'Does she know?'

'I'm not sure. We never talk about it.'

'Never?'

'She doesn't want to. That was one of the things I wanted to say.'

'Why did nobody tell me?' Adele was rigid, squeezing her handbag under her arm. 'Your father should have told me.'

'I thought you said he'd written to you?'

'He did. But he didn't tell me it was like this.'

'Are you sure?'

Crimson blotches flowered in Adele's cheeks. 'For God's sake, darling,' she said furiously, 'I did read the letter.'

'Perhaps he thought . . . I don't know. Perhaps he thought you'd be able to get here before this.'

'But he knew I was going away.' Adele was breathing quickly, opening her bag and stabbing her glasses into it.

'Mama.' Francis stepped towards her. He wanted to protect her, but didn't know how to begin.

'But my baby! My little baby!' Two tears rolled out of her eyes and exploded on the tarmac. She took a slow shuddering breath as though preparing to dive underwater.

'It's nobody's fault,' Francis said tentatively, laying one arm round his mother's shoulders. She collapsed against him, and wetness sprang through his shirt. 'Darling, I'm so sorry,' she moaned. 'So sorry. It's just that I had no idea how I ought . . .'

'Don't; there's no need.' Francis was shocked to hear how stern he sounded.

'But I feel so *ashamed*.'

'Come on. She's waiting.'

'I haven't got a hanky.'

Francis delved in a pocket. 'Pretty disgusting, I'm afraid.'

There was a soaked chuckle. 'Wouldn't know it was yours if it wasn't, would I?' She blew her nose daintily. 'Hang on. I can't go in like this.' She dabbed her eyes.

'Of course you can.'

She squeezed her lips together then relaxed them, pouting a little. 'How's that?'

'You look lovely.'

'Do I?' She twinkled at him. 'Thank you, darling. You look nice too. It's so nice seeing you in normal clothes, not those dreary old suits.'

At the door to Catherine's room Francis stood aside. 'I'll make us some coffee,' he mumbled.

Adele ignored him, sobbed 'Babykin!' and rushed past him.

'I bring you the head of John the Baptist.' Francis flourished the tray and heeled the door shut.

'Delish,' Adele beamed from the pink chair. Her eyes were sore again, and she was clutching a ball of tissue.

'I hope you haven't heard all the Greek stories without me,' he said, sitting on the bed beside Catherine and holding her cup.

'Look at you two together,' said Adele. 'I really must come and see you again soon and bring a camera. You look so perfect.'

'Romeo and Juliet,' Catherine said wearily.

'Crosse and Blackwell.'

'How do you know Crosse was a boy?' Catherine asked.

'He isn't. Blackwell is. Bryant and May.'

'Bryant's a hermaphrodite.'

'Oh yes. Sorry, I forgot. Hillard and Botting.'

'Botting's queer.'

Francis groaned. 'Well, he won't do then.' There was a silence and he looked outside to the chestnut. In past years, when the field had been rented by a local farmer, cows had grazed the lowest branches level except for one which sagged down like a power cable.

'I expect you've had masses of visitors, haven't you?' Adele was light and skittish.

'Well, yes, a few. A few regulars,' Francis answered. 'But we're all right, aren't we?'

Catherine took a deep breath. 'F looks after me like Florence Nightingale.'

'The laddie with the lamp, that's me.'

'You've got masses of get-wells, anyway.' Adele snooped among the cards on the mantelpiece. 'Not many from boys, darling. Not one that isn't a relation.'

Catherine blinked at Francis so slowly he thought she might be falling asleep. 'No,' he said jauntily. 'But she had a letter from my friend Keith, you remember.'

'Oh yes, I did meet him, didn't I? Nice boy. Nice looking.'

'Well it's the last letter from him I will get,' said Catherine.

'What do you mean?' Francis asked.

'I didn't write back. You know I didn't. You'd have posted it for me.'

'It's a pity you can't have him to stay,' said Adele, throwing her tissue into the grate.

'We could,' Francis said, 'but we haven't asked him.'

'We haven't talked about it,' said Catherine.

'I must say,' said Francis abruptly, 'I don't think it's a very good idea.'

'Listen to him!' Adele laughed. 'I see what you mean about Florence Nightingale. The scourge of Scutari.'

'Well, he's right of course,' Catherine said meekly. 'It would be dull for Keith here.'

'Which reminds me,' said Francis. 'Mama says that Czechoslovakia has been invaded.'

Adele sank back into her chair. 'Yes. I heard it on the radio. Terrible. Tanks. Gunfire. You could hear everything.'

Catherine's eyes were shut. Francis twiddled her hair behind her ears, then whispered to Adele, 'She does this – just drops off without warning. What would you like to do? I could show you the garden, or we could just sit next door if you liked.'

'A little drink?' Adele pecked Catherine on the forehead. 'Shall we draw the curtains?'

'We don't usually.'

Adele tugged her jacket down over a belt of bare brown skin. 'Oh well, let's not then,' she said, suddenly tetchy. 'Let's do what you usually do.'

★

Catherine was still asleep when Adele said she must leave. 'You're sure she'll understand?' she asked Francis for the second time, handing back her empty glass on the doorstep. They had been sitting in what the brigadier called 'the sun trap' – a patio on the garden side of the house.

'Of course, but are you sure you won't stay for lunch?'

'I never have lunch these days, so no, thank you, darling.'

'You could watch me. Dad won't be back for ages, if that's what you're thinking.'

'I wasn't. It's just the traffic, you know, and things . . . When I come down next we'll try and get out, won't we? Promise?'

'She does have some days better than others.'

'Well, I think you're being marvellous, Effie. Marvellous. I feel very proud of you.' Adele kissed him on the cheek and he slid one arm around her, bumping his finger-ends against a hard little buckle inside her coat. He wanted to tell her something, but he couldn't remember what it was.

'It was lovely to see you,' he said, clearing his throat like his father.

Adele dived into the car. 'Be sure and give her a goodbye kiss from me, won't you? And tell her to get better for our day out.' She accelerated down the drive with the choke full out, the exhaust dribbling.

Francis let himself into the field and walked towards the chestnut. He trod on a short stick and it sprang up at him like a cobra. Christ. What did she mean, accusing him of not having told her about Catherine. 'I'm her *mother*.' He put his left foot on the stick and kicked it with his right. It struggled without breaking, unbalancing him. He kicked again, and this time it lashed away through the grass. He ducked into the bell of the chestnut.

The leaves glowed so luxuriously it was like entering a marquee. There was the square white house in front of him, in another world, and the thin arm of the garden curling round it inside the fatter arm of the field. It had looked like this all his life, and now it would never be the same again.

He saw blood oozing through the grass around him like marsh-water, and the dazzling house shattering and collapsing. But there was nothing like that about Catherine; nothing violent. She was like a statue wearing down in the weather, or snow melting. She was pure and gradual.

What had Rex said about death? Those whom the gods love die young? It was easy to see why people believed that. Francis strode away from the tree into the field and stopped near the centre, his hands clenched in his pockets. How did you know what to believe if you didn't know what to feel? Looking ahead over the gentle roll of the grass, he imagined his life as a map. It was an island. Here and there, like the names of towns, were a few important events. A trip abroad. The brigadier buying them a pony. Catherine's illness. The map dissolved. At the far end of the field, sunlight flicked a car in the lane. Its engine snarled as the driver changed gear, then dwindled downhill from the village.

Somewhere Adele was sitting in her Mini listening to the radio and somewhere else tanks were trundling through narrow streets. In cobbled squares, dark coats scurried for shelter or darted into grey light to hurl a blazing bottle. There was the pop of glass exploding and the smack of gunfire. Somewhere else again, Keith was sitting under the tree by the lake. In a minute Keith would tell him to roll over, and there would be the contemptuous shot of spit. His cock squirmed and he looked across to the house. Mrs Banyard was carrying a white bundle into the garden by the sun trap. She shook it out; it was a tablecloth. Button-eyed birds would be rustling in the laurel bush behind her.

'There you are!' Mrs Banyard's voice was surprisingly loud. 'Catherine's awake. Will you be coming in, she wondered.'

'I'm on my way,' Francis shouted.

Mrs Banyard disappeared and he broke into a run, his shoes whacking the grass.

Adele's letter came two days later.

Darlings – So wonderful to see you, in the old home and all. Very keen to come again soonest now I'm back. It really doesn't take a minute with the new bypasses and whatnot. How about next Tuesday? I'll arrive around eleven unless I hear. You'll think of places we might go. I'm sure out would be easiest – and more fun! Effie look after C, C look after yourself – Effie you'll be all right, won't you! All love, A. xxx

'Something interesting?' The brigadier was halfway down the hall.

'It's from Mum actually.'

'It's got here jolly soon, hasn't it? Perhaps she posted it on the way home.'

'She couldn't very well have written it before she got here, could she?' Francis laughed uncertainly. 'Perhaps you ought to read it, Dad. She wants to take us out, Catherine and me.'

'Out? You mean out of the house?'

'Yes. I think so.'

'Got you.' The brigadier frowned. 'Let's go and be comfortable, shall we? Can't see a thing like this.' He pushed open the sitting-room door and sunlight blared at them through the french windows. Francis sat on the arm of a sofa. The brigadier spent most of his time in this room, but the cushions in the deep armchair were so proudly plumped it was difficult to imagine anyone ever sat on them. Let alone sat on them day after day, evening after evening. The only signs of life were two shallow dents in the powder-blue tapestry covering a long footstool. Dad's heels, Francis said to himself. Jesus. Poor Dad.

'Well. It's friendly,' said the brigadier, handing the letter back.

'But there's not a hope of us going. It's a crazy idea.'

'I wouldn't say that altogether.'

'But you know how Cath is, Dad,' Francis protested. 'She's asleep all the time.'

The brigadier fingered his moustache. 'Your mother's a very strong-minded woman.'

'But Catherine . . .' There was a squeak of desperation in Francis' voice. 'I thought you wouldn't want us to go.'

'It's not that I want you to go . . .'

'Well then.'

'I'm not making myself clear, am I?' The brigadier turned to the window and the hard sky made his face a silhouette. 'I don't want to trouble you with everything,' he said placidly. 'You've got enough on your plate as it is. But I thought while your mother was here the other day – I thought I'd go and see Catherine's doctor and have a real chat to him. You know; away from here, to see how we really were.'

'And?'

'We had a proper session, and he's very pleased with her, very pleased. And she's very brave. But he says we must prepare ourselves.'

Francis nodded sluggishly.

'Well, that's what I mean about going out, you see?' The brigadier stepped forward as if the conversation could now end.

'I'm sorry, Dad, I don't really see.'

'No.' The brigadier didn't sound surprised. 'Well, the thing is, the doctor thinks Catherine ought to go into hospital. He feels we can't look after her properly any more ourselves, because she's in a lot of pain and she needs a lot of nursing.'

'But we can't let her go now – we just can't!' Francis heard a voice from a long time ago saying angrily, 'How could you?' It was Adele's.

'Steady on,' said the brigadier, still calm and level. 'I agree absolutely – we can't let her go. I said as much to the doctor.

He admits having her in hospital won't do much good, so what's the point, eh? But just to be on the safe side I said: what about us hiring a nurse, and he said good idea. I know it's an invasion.'

Francis smiled weakly. 'It's better than hospital.'

'Precisely so. Anyway, I thought no time like the present, and went round the corner to some agency place he recommended, and told them what we wanted. I must say they were jolly nice. Jolly efficient. They're sending someone out over the next couple of days. I'll warn Ma Banyard. We don't want her nose put out of joint. And I don't want it to bother Catherine. I don't want her . . .'

Francis interrupted him: 'I see about the day out.'

'I think Normal Services, don't you?'

'If you can call a visit from Mother normal.'

'Now now,' said the brigadier implacably, and perched on an arm of his chair. His face looked scorched, as if he'd opened the door of an oven and stared in. 'If she's not up to it you can always re-schedule,' he went on. 'Or I can pop out again. But I think it's a good idea, going. In fact, I can't think why I haven't thought of it myself. It must be very dull for you here.'

'No it isn't,' Francis burst out, imploring. 'Not at all.' He wanted to say more, but couldn't think. He stared into the field. A breeze had sprung up and cloud-shadows were sliding smartly over the grass.

'Shall we go and put it to Catherine, then?'

Francis searched his father's face. 'Yes. Thanks, Dad.'

The brigadier smiled politely and flinched away. 'Don't thank me,' he said softly. 'Nothing to thank me for.' He smoothed the arm of his chair, then the arm of the sofa, just as Francis imagined he must do at the end of every day before going to bed.

The nurse, Mrs Underhill, was American. The brigadier liked her and so did Francis. She moved in two days after her interview. Catherine was suspicious and told her to wear ordinary clothes, not her blue uniform.

'I can't think why you and Dad are so keen on her,' she said later, when Francis was eating his lunch from a tray in the pink chair.

'Cath, we've been through this,' Francis said wanly.

'No we haven't. She's only just got here.'

'We need her in case anything happens.'

'What sort of thing?'

'Don't be difficult. Medical things. She's got that wheel-chair contraption, for instance.'

'I don't need it,' Catherine winced. 'Where is she now?'

'In the kitchen, with Dad and Mrs Banyard.'

'I don't want her sitting in here.'

'She won't sit in here. She's got a chair in her own room.'

'I want to go on just as we have been.'

'So do I.' Francis lifted a forkful of peas to his mouth. 'But she does seem a nice cheery sort.'

'A nice cheery sort?' Catherine's voice was like water dropped on a hotplate. 'Well I don't like her. I don't like her fat arms. And her legs don't reach the ground when she sits down.'

'Don't be ridiculous. She can't help her legs.' Francis pushed his food to the side of his plate. 'Now, what can I get you?'

'Nothing.' Catherine rolled her head from side to side like a child in a rage, and Francis stood up. He put one hand at the top of her spine and bent her forwards, flipping over the topmost pillow in the bank behind her and smoothing it. Then he lowered her gently back. There were large flakes of dandruff in her hair.

'You're the best nurse,' she whispered with her eyes shut. 'We don't need another one.'

A little salty wave broke through Francis' chest and died in his throat. 'Just have a zizz,' he said carefully. 'I won't be far away.'

On the morning of Adele's visit, Catherine's clothes were draped on the arm of the pink chair. 'It's like Christmas,' she said after breakfast. 'Having my clothes laid out like that.'

'Mrs Underhill did it last night.'

Catherine's eyes glittered. 'Will you help me dress?'

'What, now? We're not due to go for another couple of hours.'

'No I know, but still. Please.'

'If you want, then, OK. I'll just take your tray through.'

By the time he returned Catherine had stripped off her nightdress and wriggled into her pants. She was sitting on the edge of the bed with her back to him, her unbrushed hair straggling over her shoulders.

Francis knelt to pull her jeans up her legs. 'I'm sorry.' She mumbled; she sounded ashamed.

'Don't. Don't say that.'

'Don't be cross.'

'Christ, Catherine, I'm not cross.' His hands were trembling, and when she stuck out an arm so that he could slide on the sleeve of her shirt, he glimpsed her rib-cage like two clawmarks and her sore-looking strawberry nipples. He sank back on to his haunches; he felt exhausted.

'Put on my other sleeve, for Jesus' sake,' Catherine hissed. Her eyes were clenched, and she was twisting her shirt-tail to cover herself.

'We don't have to go,' Francis whispered. 'We could change our minds and stay here. Everyone would understand.'

'Please, F. I want to go.' She popped her eyes open suddenly and he rocked backwards, clutching at her knees. Her legs were so thin he thought he was putting his hands directly on to her bones.

'Careful!' she gasped, then collected herself. 'I'm not a well girl.'

Francis hung his head. 'Why don't I leave you in peace until it's time?'

Catherine smiled and closed her eyes and said nothing.

★

Adele trilled 'Yoohoo' in the hall.

'What's happening?' Catherine woke up, confused.

'She's here.'

'Are we going?'

'We're going. OK?'

Adele appeared before Catherine could answer, and kissed them both like a bird stabbing for worms. 'Catherine, darling, you look marvellous.'

'So do you.'

Adele was wearing a black shirt and trousers, and her sunglasses were nesting in her hair. 'It's a bit funereal, I'm afraid,' she giggled. 'Where are we off to?'

'Bradwell,' said Francis.

'Where?'

'Bradwell-on-Sea,' he said robustly. 'Or rather: Bradwell-juxta-Mare. It's beyond Maldon. Not far.'

Adele frowned. 'Doesn't that MP live there, that queer one? What's he called?'

'Tom Driberg. Yes; but don't worry, we're not going to see him.'

'Oh, I'd rather like to. The thing about queers is, they're always very nice to women. I'm rather partial to them.' She giggled again.

'There's a power-station there too,' said Francis. 'But we're not going to see that, either.'

'What does that leave?'

'It's a surprise.'

'You'll have to map-read then, darling. I'm absolutely . . .' Adele broke off as Mrs Underhill tilted her plump face into the room.

Adele immediately stuck out her hand. 'Hallo, I'm Catherine's and Effie's mother.'

Mrs Underhill bobbed. 'How do you do? I just wanted to see everything was OK before you go . . .'

'You're an American?' Adele interrupted.

'Yes, ma'am,' drawled Mrs Underhill playfully. 'From Utah.'

70

'How interesting.'

'This is Mrs Underhill, Catherine's nurse,' said Francis, blushing. 'We're fine, thanks. We're just off.'

'Catherine's nurse,' Adele crooned. 'I didn't know.'

'I'm sure I told you, Mother,' Francis said.

'I'm sure you didn't.'

'Well, we can tell you all about Mrs Underhill in the car,' said Catherine. 'Now come on.'

'Have you got a woolly, dear?'

'She's taking one,' said Francis. 'She won't wear it. It's a lovely day.'

'It's colder than it looks.' Mrs Underhill shook her head and her jowls trembled. 'Don't think I'm interfering.'

'Yes,' said Catherine, glaring.

They squeezed out of the room, Francis supporting Catherine on his arm. She slithered into the back seat of the Mini as though she were a scarf he had thrown there. 'Why don't you lie across it?' he asked, unfolding a rug over her legs.

'I won't need this. I'll be fine. I'll be sick if I sit sideways.' Her voice was high and thin with excitement.

Mrs Underhill was trying to fit the wheelchair into the boot and he went to help her. 'Oh no,' she was moaning. 'Oh no, it won't go. I thought it would go folded up. Oh no.'

'Don't worry,' he said briskly. 'I'll carry her if need be.'

'Just come on, will you,' Catherine said. 'Get in. Let's just go, can't we?'

He climbed in beside Adele and as they moved off shouted, 'Goodbye, Mrs Underhill. See you later.'

'Good riddance,' said Catherine.

'Funny woman,' said Adele.

'Just shy, I think,' said Francis.

'Francis likes her.' Catherine's voice was faint.

'Not especially. I just don't not like her, that's all.'

'Come on, you two,' Adele flexed her arms on the steering wheel. 'There's a map somewhere, Effie.'

Francis opened the atlas on his knee as they drove through the village. It was weeks since he had been even this far from the house, and Adele's Mini, scooting close to the road, made everything seem colossal. Huge, heavy-headed grasses spurted out of the hedges and hissed beside the car in a long breaking wave. A bramble thwacked its arthritic finger against his door. The warm wind battered his cheek.

'Is this window too much for you?' He twisted round to look at Catherine. She had pulled the rug up to her chin and her hair was streaming back from her face. A blurred red bar lined her cheeks, as if her bones were warming up.

She shook her head. 'I like it.'

Francis stretched over the back of his seat and gently squeezed her bare ankle.

'Help!' squeaked Adele. 'T-junction! Map-reader!'

After a few miles Francis gave up trying to make himself heard above the engine, except when Adele asked the way. At first the country seemed to be playing tricks on him. He had lived in this part of Essex all his life and recognized every tree, every track leading off the road. Yet they looked foreign to him. Who owned these fields? When he and Catherine had ridden across them as children, each one had seemed a part of home. Now they looked trussed up and separate.

The Mini flashed past the dark entrance to a lane; he knew it led to the Grange, where they had been to parties at Christmas, but now the opening looked impassable, and the pines beside it skeletal and forbidding. It was the same when they wriggled through villages. In Coggershall he glanced sideways and found himself staring at a grey-brick house across a courtyard. Behind the house, dwarfing it, was the mountainous corrugated wall of a barn. It was Kings, the grain merchant, where Francis had worked for a fortnight last summer during harvest, and where he knew people. Today it had nothing to do with him. The black windows winked in the grey house and were gone.

As they moved south-east, through Maldon and along the Blackwater estuary, things began to change. Francis let his mind free-wheel. It must have something to do with money, this difference. Out here, instead of big immaculate fields, there were thin gulleys of grazing reaching down to the water, or stockades of young firs around caravan sites. Everything still seemed private, but Francis thought he might be able to have part of it, if he wanted.

'Oh dear.' Adele nodded towards a railway truck in a bald meadow. As Francis looked, one of its doors opened and a young man, stripped to the waist, holding a gleaming grainscoop and smiling to himself, stepped out into the sun.

Francis smiled too. 'There's a lot of chicken abuse down these parts,' he said.

'Still,' Adele said blankly, 'he seems happy enough.'

Francis wondered whether she had heard him, and stared at the estuary. Wide black sheets of mud stretched beside the water, with here and there a beached boat, or a litter of gulls. The river was a lugubrious trickle. He imagined a page in a book, with a block of millennia divided into different coloured bands, like layers of rock. Then he imagined a fleet of Viking ships with striped sails.

'Penny for them,' said Catherine. Her head was tilted against the window, and she had slipped one hand between her cheek and the shaking glass.

'The Battle of Maldon. Do you want a cushion?'

'No thanks. Boys' history.'

'What are you two on about?' Adele asked.

'Vikings,' said Francis. 'You're doing jolly well. Another quarter of an hour.'

'How's the invalid?' Adele asked the mirror.

'Yes.'

'Delightful vistas your brother has laid on for us.'

'I love it.'

Francis tried to remember whether there would be a full, wide view of the sea when they reached the coast, but there was only ever the estuary, broadening slowly, deep enough now in the centre to float a few small sailing boats.

Then the hills were behind them and they darted into Bradwell.

'*Voilà*,' said Adele, and bibbed the horn. 'Where now?'

They were beside a red-brick church-tower. 'Left here. *Here.*'

Adele threw herself sideways as though cornering at high speed and made the noise of squealing rubber.

'Very good!' Francis laughed.

'My driving or my squealing?'

'Your squealing. Well, both.' Francis laid his open hand on her thigh. 'That must be Driberg's house.'

'God! Gloomy! Those trees!'

'They're to hide unspeakable acts.'

'What do you know about unspeakable acts?'

'It's got Angelica Kauffmann ceilings,' Catherine interrupted.

'How do you know *that*?' Francis asked, taking his hand off Adele.

'I read it somewhere.'

'Get you.'

'Get him, more likely.'

Francis clicked his tongue. He knew almost nothing about Driberg, but the brigadier had once shared a compartment with him on the train to London, and referred to him as 'that dodgy bugger the MP'. He grinned as the house and its barricade of trees sank behind the wall of a school playground.

'And now,' he announced, in a silly clipped voice, 'an altogether different and more charming prospect. Bradwell power-station. Massive and concrete. Brings power to the people. Well worth a turn of the head.'

A gigantic cube darkened the left-hand half of the sky. It seemed to be permanently in shadow, and to cast twilight all around it, making it impossible to see any details: no windows, no iron zigzag ladders, no signs.

'Honestly, darling,' said Adele, 'what a hideous place.'

Francis was suddenly unnerved. 'Well,' he shrugged, 'with a bit of luck we won't see it when we're at the church.'

'A church?' Adele repeated, disappointed. 'Is that what we're seeing?'

74

'Yes,' said Francis, 'and I think this is the turning.' They had reached a wide gateway scarred with tyre tracks. To one side was a fingerpost which read: 'St Peter-on-the-wall. C.7 church'.

'*Seventh* century?' said Adele. 'That must be a mistake. Seventeenth century it must mean.'

'No,' Francis insisted. 'That's right. Seventh. And it's got the ruin of some Roman thing round it. Except I don't think you can see that.' He spoke over his shoulder. 'What does Miss Kauffmann think?'

'I think,' said Catherine through clenched teeth, 'unless you go a bit slower I'm going to throw up.'

'Sorry, darling.' Adele laughed and the Mini dawdled the last hundred yards, stopping at an iron gate. The church stood ahead of them, at the end of a track running between a hedge and a stubble field.

'Is that it?' Adele turned off the engine. 'It's not much to look at.'

Francis said nothing, and turned to Catherine. She was wedged into the corner, her head slumped on to her chest.

'Let's go,' she said hoarsely. 'I'm ready.'

While Francis hoisted Catherine out of the car, Adele fiddled with the chain on the gate. 'Oh, help, I can't do it,' she blathered.

Francis propped Catherine against the bonnet like a bundle of sticks. 'OK for a second?'

'Sure.' Her head lolled back. 'I can smell the sea.'

Francis murmured impatiently in Adele's ear: 'You'll have to close it behind us because I'm going to have to carry her. All right? Can you do that?' He turned away before she could answer and swept Catherine up in his arms.

She laid her head on his shoulder. 'Get me to the church on time.' The ghost of a giggle ran through her.

With Adele traipsing along behind, clutching her glossy handbag, Francis felt ridiculous and powerful. He was a giant striding across the baked-mud canyons which were the entire world of some diminutive species. Yet he was part of this species, too. He imagined the three of them from the air, lurching like desperate insects across the final strip of earth towards the sea. He could see the water clearly now – a bright gash with the church outlined against it: a square brick shed, a commonplace red roof.

'Well done, he-man,' panted Adele, toiling up beside him. 'Can't say I think much of your edifice, though, even if it is old. Looks like a barn to me.'

'Can I get down?' Catherine slid out of Francis' arms, leaning against him.

He was breathing heavily. 'I think it *was* used as a barn for a bit, as a matter of fact.'

'There wouldn't have been room for much. You'd have trouble getting even a tractor in.'

'I don't think the Saxons had many tractors,' Francis said truculently, shouldering the door open.

'Morning.' A man's voice floated towards them.

Adele pushed past into the chilly half-light, her shoes clicking on the plain slabs. 'I'm so sorry. We didn't know there was anyone here. Is it all right if we look round?'

'It's not my church,' said the man. A pair of binoculars glinted round his neck.

Adele stood beside him in front of the altar. 'This is my son and daughter,' she announced. 'We've driven over from the other side of Essex to have a look.'

The man screwed up his eyes at Francis and Catherine, then stared into the roof. There was scrawny, chicken's skin on his neck. 'Not much to see, but what there is is worth it,' he said to no one in particular.

'Can we sit down?' Catherine slid on to a bench inside the door where the sun lay over their knees like a rug.

'Like the man says,' Francis muttered. 'Not much to see.' Four small massively-framed windows trickled light down the bare brick walls. The only decoration was above the altar – a wooden cross with a life-sized Christ on it.

'Look where all the windows and doors were,' said Catherine. 'Look over there. Something's smashed right through and they've had to build it from scratch.'

Francis was listening to the sea outside, sighing on the mud.

'Happy?' Catherine asked. Muscle bubbled in the line of her jaw.

'It's wonderful here. Wonderful. It feels . . .'

'Darlings.' Adele's voice bounced at them. 'This nice man has asked me to go and look at some duck for a minute. He's got a hutch just around the corner.'

'A *hide*.' The stranger's voice was strangled. 'I've got a *hide* here. I work for the Trust.'

'We won't go far,' Catherine said.

'Sure you don't mind then?' Adele and the man disappeared into the sunlight, and dust danced in the open doorway.

'Can we go up for a moment?' Catherine asked.

'To the altar? Why not.' Francis offered his arm.

'Look at that,' Catherine sank on to another bench and stared at the crucifix. The Christ was painted on planks as thick as railway sleepers. He was lifting his arms primly, and his knees were pressed together. His face was as smooth as a spoon.

'He doesn't seem to realize he's being crucified,' said Francis.

'How do you mean?'

'He doesn't look as though it hurts.'

'That's the point, isn't it?'

'Is it? Silly me.' Francis was embarrassed, but Catherine seemed not to have heard.

'The point is: people can sit here and just feel for themselves. The blanker his face is, the easier it is for people. They can just put on it whatever they want. Whatever they're feeling.'

'Faith, hope and charity,' said Francis sensibly, but his voice sounded hollow.

'Well, yes. Or sorrow. Or pain. Or fear.' Catherine

coughed and Francis took her hand, rubbing away the wet blobs of her saliva.

'I didn't mean to be facetious.'

'Facetious? You didn't sound facetious.'

A breeze waltzed through the door and faded. Francis swallowed. 'Well, go on then,' he said.

The muscle bubbled back into Catherine's jaw. 'I don't know what there is to say, really. I know what I'm supposed to say. I'm supposed to let him feel for me. That's why his face is blank – so that I can write on it. We learn that in Scripture.'

'God, we don't.' He gave a gurgling laugh.

Catherine ignored him. 'But the point is: I can't.' She snatched her hand away. 'Don't,' she gulped, suddenly furious. 'Just don't. Don't touch me.'

Francis gaped at her. 'Please, Cath. Please don't cry.'

'I bloody well want to cry,' she spat at him. 'I never bloody well cry. Not once. Can't you see? I know what's happening and I can't talk about it to anyone, not even to you. I've got to be with you all the time, so I can't talk about it to you. Do you understand?'

'Yes,' Francis said blindly.

'But I must talk to somebody.' Catherine's voice was sloshing out of her, and jagged blotches had burst into her face.

'Do you mean God?'

'Of course I mean God. I see that blank face, and I try and see things in it, and I can't. I can't make anything stick. I can't find anywhere to put my feelings.' She pitched forward and Francis heard, 'Oh Christ.' It was his own voice, but he wasn't sure whether he had spoken aloud. Catherine's shoulders twitched violently under his arm. He wanted to put both arms round her, but somehow it was impossible.

'I'm scared,' she said in a drab, level breath, her head sunk between her shoulders. 'Scared.' She slapped both hands over her face, then peeled them away. Her anger had left her. 'And what do you think?' she asked calmly, like someone speaking under hypnosis.

Francis was baffled; he felt he hadn't been paying attention and had lost his place in the story. 'What do I think?'

'What do you think about death?' she asked, in the same flat voice.

He looked across the church at a bricked-in doorway. 'I don't know.'

'You must think something. I thought you and Keith Ogilvie talked about this sort of thing all the time, you're so brainy.'

Francis couldn't think who she meant. Then the lean, olive face swam into his head, severe, saying: 'We mustn't be sentimental.' 'Keith's got no time for death,' he said.

Catherine paused then repeated. 'I see. Keith's got no time for death.'

'That's not . . . he doesn't . . .'

'And that means you don't have time for it either, is that right?'

Francis was winded. 'No, Cath, you know that's not true. It's just that I don't know.' He breathed deeply. 'It's just that I haven't reached any conclusions yet.'

'Well, do you believe in God, then?' Catherine demanded. She had braced her arms on her knees and was facing him.

'I don't know that either. Sometimes I do, yes.'

'F, I'm asking you, please.' He felt a spurt of relief. She needed his help. He opened his mouth without any idea of what he might say. 'Whenever I've believed in God I haven't needed to,' he heard. 'There's been nothing to worry about, or ask for. Now I do have things to ask for, I don't believe in him.'

'What do you mean when you say God?' Catherine was clipped and impersonal.

'I mean whether there's life after death. Other things, too, but mainly that.'

'And you don't believe those things now?'

'In the past I have done, when I didn't care much. But not now, no.'

'Not at all?'

'No. I think when we die we just go out. That's it. I think I'm a sort of higher bug – I think we all are.'

'Thank you,' Catherine said quietly, and folded her arms.

'Just because I think that,' Francis floundered, 'it doesn't mean it's true. Sometimes I worry I haven't got any feelings, and that's why I don't believe in God any more.'

Catherine shook her head.

Francis grinned at her nervously. 'Well, it would have been more feeling of me if I'd told you I did believe in God, wouldn't it?'

'I don't want charity. Soft soap.'

'I might change my mind.'

'You might,' Catherine smiled as if nothing mattered. 'I wonder where our dear mother has got to?'

Francis cleared his throat. 'We didn't have to come all this way to have this conversation, you know. You will talk again, won't you, if you want to? At home?'

'I didn't know we were going to have it. It just happened. But thanks, anyway.' Catherine was still smiling vacantly. Then her hand scuttled on to his like a crab climbing a stone. 'Let's go.'

Francis scooped her up in his arms and carried her down the church into the sun. She buried her face against his neck. 'Blinding!'

'You'll get used to it in a minute.' He blinked round him at the stubble, the blue sea beyond a fringe of reeds.

'Smell that salt.'

'And that mud.' With his feet apart, leaning slightly backwards to take Catherine's weight, Francis wasn't a giant any more, or an insect, he was someone carrying a victim away from a massacre. The ancient stones of the church bounced their heat on to his back, warming him. He had escaped something.

Then Catherine mumbled into his collar and his elation left him.

'What?' he asked, his heart rattling.

'I said: I felt beaten.'

'Beaten?' Francis gazed at a ridge in the grass ahead of them. It was part of the Roman fort; he hadn't noticed it on their way in. When the breeze pressed down, the grass turned silver. 'What do you mean, beaten?'

'I mean I ache. Everything aches.' She squinted into his face, too close to see clearly.

'I'll take you to the car.'

As Francis carried her, he wondered why he didn't collapse. Or scream. It was disgraceful, shameful, just to keep walking when Catherine would never see any of this again. They passed a young oak in the hedge beside the track. Ivy was flaming up the trunk; its dark-green leaves were veined with yellow, and every one looked like a brooch. He wanted to rip a strand away, and take it home to study it.

When they reached the car Catherine slipped into the back seat without a word, and pulled the rug up to her chin. She was panting.

'I'll just get Adele.'

'She's coming,' Catherine breathed. 'Look. Round the church.'

Francis jogged a few yards back down the track, then put his hands to his mouth and shouted: 'Adele!'

'C-o-m-i-n-g.' Her voice seesawed like a child's, and she shook the stranger's hand.

Francis saw their bright clasp against the black cavern of the open door. He saw the entire little church behind them, ragged and golden in the sun, and beyond the church, the sea. The water had swollen; puddles shone among the reeds, and half a dozen mallard, surprised by something invisible, sprayed steeply away from him, honking like cars. He looked back to Adele. She had released the stranger's hand and was patting his binoculars.

'Jesus.' Francis seethed under his breath, then shouted again: 'Come on, Mother. Now.' He turned savagely towards the Mini, scouring the dusty windscreen for Catherine's face. She seemed to be already asleep, her head tilted up, pale, smudged with shadows like a miniature moon.

Catherine died exactly five weeks later. Wednesday was an awkward day to die, Francis discovered. People thought the following Saturday too soon for the funeral – but if it was left until the middle of the next week, would everyone be able to get off work?

'They ought to have the chance to come, at least, don't you think?' the brigadier asked Francis. They were looking out of the window in Catherine's room; she had only been dead a few hours.

'Yes.'

'Well,' the brigadier coaxed. 'Why don't we say this Saturday and be done with it?'

Francis nodded.

'I'm sure that's right. I'll get on the blower straight away, and sort out one or two things. We ought to put it in the papers. Perhaps you'd like to come to the vicarage with me this evening, so we can talk about the service?' The brigadier wiped his nose with a big yellow handkerchief. 'What will you do now?'

'Tidy up here, I think.'

'Don't worry about that. Mrs Underhill can do that.'

'I'd like to.'

'Well, if you want. Don't overdo it.' As the brigadier turned to go, light picked up the serrated line on his florid cheek where his razor had stopped. His eyes were set in furry hollows, and brimming with liquid, but there was no trace of tears in his voice; he sounded keen. 'I'll be getting along then,' he said. 'You know where I am.'

'Yes, Dad,' Francis said. 'Thanks.' He followed his father to the door, closed it quickly and leant against it. Ever since the previous evening, when they had seen Catherine was dying, the house had been in uproar. While Francis and the brigadier had sat at the bedside, Mrs Banyard and Mrs Underhill had been clattering in the kitchen. Every so often one of them would appear with a cup of tea, but their noise sounded more like spring-cleaning. When Catherine had stopped breathing, just before six, the hiss of her last breath was lost in the crash of a baking-tin rattling on to the kitchen lino. 'Oh, shut up,' the brigadier had said, and then, 'Oh Catherine. Oh God.' He had folded her hands together on her chest and crossed himself. Francis had never seen his father cross himself.

The doctor had arrived immediately, as if he had been waiting at the end of the drive. He scurried about, banishing them from Catherine's room, making telephone calls. Soon two other people appeared. They had seemed to think, these sleek strangers in their white shirts and crisp trousers, that they owned Catherine. One of them asked Francis whether he would like a few minutes alone with her. He appeared to be giving permission. Shortly afterwards they had covered her face with a blanket and hoisted her on to a stretcher; then there had been the purr of an engine, and fat tyres seething over the tarmac.

Francis knelt by the bed. On Catherine's table was a pile of books, with the corner of Keith's letter sticking out of one of them. He read what he could, but it made no sense: 'In the sum . . . you once . . . end of the . . . your bro . . .' He blinked. There was Catherine's half-drunk Lucozade, with its orange bubbles still clinging to the glass; and there was the plastic spoon still smeared with her red medicine. He saw his hand ferrying the spoon to her mouth. The medicine bulged and might spill at any moment, but it never did spill, it was too gooey. He heard himself say, 'Come on. Just open a bit wider. This'll make you feel better,' and the cracked lips opened a slit.

On the bank of pillows was the cavity where Catherine's head had been. All yesterday evening her chin had sharpened until she looked like a runner stretching for the tape. Then in the small hours her expression changed. Her chin had sunk on to her chest; her mouth sagged open. She no longer looked like a runner, but like someone in a trance. A mystic. Francis had wondered whether she might blurt out her innermost secret thoughts. What would they be? Things he didn't know? Things which might hurt him? He had looked at her more closely and she changed again. For the first time in weeks she looked like herself. Like his twin. Then there had been the rattle of the baking-tin from the kitchen and she had died.

Francis pressed his face exactly into the dent on the pillow, keeping his eyes open and dragging breath in through his mouth. He discovered Catherine's sour sweat and stuck his tongue into the pillow, but there was no taste of her, just the banal cotton.

The telephone pinged across the hall and he hoisted himself to his feet. The brigadier must have finished a call. Francis moved to the end of the bed and dragged the blankets clear. He tugged the bottom sheet. A few crumbs and hairs trampolined.

The brigadier cleared his throat in the doorway. 'Getting on all right?'

'Fine thanks, Dad. Just doing the bed. Not making much headway, I'm afraid.'

'I rang your mother.'

Francis began to fold a blanket, not looking at his father. 'I was just thinking someone should.'

'She's very upset of course.'

'Yes.' Francis dumped the blanket on the bed.

'She wants you to ring her.'

'Now?'

'Well, yes, but I'd give it a minute if I were you. She is very upset.'

'Poor Mother.'

'Hysterical, really.' The brigadier was almost whimsical, fingering his moustache. 'But she's got that chap with her, hasn't she?'

'Joe.'

'Yes; Joe.' The brigadier stepped forward. 'I'll just give you a hand here.' He picked up a blanket and they shyly swooped towards and away from each other like dancers.

At eleven o'clock the hearse turned into the drive. Francis ran down from his bedroom, tightening the black tie his father had lent him.

Mrs Banyard loomed in the hall holding a dumpy hat. 'That shirt needs an iron,' she complained.

'It won't show when I've got my coat on.'

'I'll do it for you,' she called after him, but he pretended he hadn't heard.

The long sides of the hearse gleamed dully. A small man wearing a grey peaked cap was standing by the car, and as Francis came up he dipped suddenly to pant on the bonnet, then rubbed away the cloud of his breath with an orange cloth. 'Sorry about that, sir,' he said perkily. 'It's the flies. They're a menace even this late in the summer. You are the young lady's brother, I assume?'

'Yes. Her twin.' Francis grimaced; he didn't want the man to know anything about him.

'Oh, that's nice, sir. Please accept my most sincere condolences.' The man nodded into the back of the hearse at a cascade of yellow and bronze flowers. 'Nice lot of tributes, anyway, for the sad occasion.'

Francis was bewildered. Under the flowers was the coffin. Catherine would never have liked wood as pale as that. It was brutal.

The brigadier appeared, four-square in a black overcoat. 'All right, old boy?'

'She's here,' Francis said uselessly.

'You just get ready, then, and we'll be off.'

Francis slipped into the hall and took the stairs two at a time. When he returned the hearse was halfway down the drive, and the brigadier was waiting in his Daimler by the doorstep. They rolled so slowly into the lane that Francis wondered whether the car would stall. 'Nasty smell of petrol,' he said.

'Mmm.' The brigadier fiddled with the choke. 'I suppose hearses have some special device, do they?'

Francis unclenched his fists. His tongue was floppy. Ready to wag, but dry. He was dry everywhere – mouth, eyes, face, the skin of his whole body. Even his insides were parched.

'Oh look,' said the brigadier, 'the Dixons.' Francis saw an elderly couple staring over a box hedge ahead of them. As the hearse drew level, Mr Dixon whisked off his faded tweed cap and pressed it to his chest. Mrs Dixon, who was wearing a pale-blue pinny, gave a demure wave, then put her hand to her mouth, aghast.

Francis gazed at the floor of the Daimler. It was speckled with grass and gravel. He could feel the Dixons close to him, as though he were passing a fire. His cheeks burned.

Then they were behind him, and he looked up. Dotted along the road to the centre of the village, other people were standing in their gardens. Francis knew most of them only slightly; some of them were new arrivals, people he had never met.

'These new buildings have fitted in very well, haven't they?' said the brigadier.

'Yes, very well,' Francis mumbled. 'Very good.' Now he could see down the village to the field at the bottom, and the church beside it. There were cars packing both sides of the street, and someone had opened the gate into the field so that more cars could line up on the grass. The church bell began to toll.

They drew up by the lych-gate. Six men in black overcoats scuttled out, and the largest of them opened the back of the hearse, laying a hand on the coffin. Another man, weedy-looking, with red eyelashes, sidled towards them and the brigadier wound down his window.

'Brigadier Mayne, sir? Good morning, sir,' said the weedy man through his nose. His thin lips twisted. 'Mr Oates. We spoke on the telephone.'

The brigadier jabbed an elbow sideways. 'This is my son, Francis.'

'Does everything seem satisfactory, sir?'

'Thank you, yes.'

Francis looked back to the hearse. The men had taken all the wreaths except one off the coffin, which they were dragging out. Mr Oates switched off his smile. 'When you're ready we can process to the church. My men will distribute the wreaths at the graveside during the service. If you would like to follow behind the coffin with your son? You'll find your wife is awaiting you in the church porch. She can join us there.'

The brigadier jerked round. 'My wife?'

'She arrived only a few moments ago, with her mother – Mrs Vaisey is it? Sadly the traffic had detained them leaving London. I took the liberty of recommending that they remain in the porch until you arrived, sir. I thought it would be out of the wind for your wife's mother.'

'Quite so.' The brigadier cranked up his window.

'He wasn't to know,' said Francis.

'No.' The brigadier seemed to have swollen in his black coat. His heavy face was suffused with blood. 'Anyway, not to worry. You just stay with me.'

'Yes, Dad.'

'Well done.' He patted Francis on the knee, and Francis thought: 'I can't remember the last time my father touched me.'

They climbed out of the car. The man beneath Catherine's left foot was several inches shorter than the others, and as the coffin shuffled towards the lych-gate, it tilted sharply towards him. Francis wondered whether the wreath would slide off, and reached up to straighten it. It was a tightly bound circle of red roses. The brigadier's square writing was on the label: 'To our darling. From her father and her twin.'

They stooped under the lych-gate into the churchyard. The flint-covered church with its little wooden steeple looked as if it had been sprinkled with sugar. Organ notes meandered towards them.

The brigadier peered round the side of the coffin like a driver wanting to overtake. 'Here we are,' he said. The vicar was billowing in the porch, clasping a prayer book to his chest. In front of him were Adele and her mother, who was bobbing from foot to foot.

'Hallo, Adele.' Francis ducked under the broad rim of her black hat and kissed her. She had pulled up her hair and looked tiny.

'Oh darling.' She pressed him away from her, and two large tears scurried out of her eyes. Then she burrowed in a small handbag. Everything about her – the bag, her strict black coat, her gleaming shoes – was brand new. 'I must be brave,' she told him. 'I promised myself I would be brave.'

'Are you all right?' Francis asked, but Adele was ignoring him, dabbing at her nose while she looked over his shoulder.

'Hallo, Edmund,' she said, gushing.

What would his father do? Francis wondered. Kiss her? Shake her hand? He was about to stand aside and watch when Adele's mother hopped in front of him. Her deeply wrinkled face looked like a cloth which had been wrung out, then hardened.

'Hallo, Granny.' When he kissed her, her face was astonishingly soft.

'Better leave those two love-birds to themselves,' she whispered loudly, pressing down her brown cloche hat.

'Hardly love-birds, Granny.'

'It's never too late to try again. Your grandfather and I were passionate to the end. To the end.'

Francis glanced at the coffin, and imagined Catherine smiling in the darkness. He heard her voice saying, 'What did I tell you? Completely barking.'

'Of course it's terribly sad,' Mrs Vaisey went on. 'Terribly. Tragic.'

'Do you think we ought to go in?'

'I think the vicar's telling your father. He seems such a nice man.'

'The vicar?'

'Oh Francis,' cackled Mrs Vaisey, reeling backwards as though Francis had struck her. 'Of course the vicar. Here's your father now.'

'Hallo, Granny V,' the brigadier said stoutly. 'Very good of you to come.' He shook her hand and her shrunken body jerked up and down inside her coat.

'Hallo, Edmund, you look blooming.'

'I keep pretty fit.'

'But of course it is terribly sad. I was just saying to Catherine. Terribly sad. Tragic.'

'To Francis,' said Francis.

'Yes, to Francis.' Mrs Vaisey's eyes narrowed suspiciously.

'I think we might go in, don't you? I think we're all ready.'

The vicar swept up, flattening his long thin coil of hair round his scalp. 'Good morning, Francis. Your father has discussed the procession with you, has he? You and him together, then your mother and Mrs Vaisey here. All right?' He flapped away into the porch and opened the double doors.

The organ immediately began a slow march and the congregation rose. Francis stepped to his father's side. Adele sniffed behind them. Then the coffin lurched forwards and Francis bumped against his father's arm, gazing at the invisible ground beneath his feet.

When the service was over everyone formed a wide semicircle around Catherine's grave. Francis was jostled by his father and mother to within a few feet of the hole; its sides were dark chocolate, patterned with gleaming squares where the spade had cut sharply. Hunks and crumbs of mud were scattered on the surrounding grass, but the main bulk had been piled in a neat hump and covered with a green tarpaulin.

The coffin stretched beside the grave with three broad canvas straps underneath it. The vicar stood at its head, holding an open prayer book. His voice sighed and sank, making his words incomprehensible, and when the under-takers suddenly sprang forwards, picked up the canvas straps and lowered the coffin into the hole, Francis felt cheated. Surely it wasn't time for that yet? The semi-circle stiffened as though someone was expected to jump into the grave, yelling. Francis craned his neck. Greenfly had appeared on one of the roses. Then the straps snaked out of the grave, and the undertakers shrank away.

There was a hollow pattering and the vicar wiped one hand on his thigh, under his surplice. His words began to surge and sink again. A breeze skipped up the field beyond the graveyard, whitening the grass. A rook cawed. 'It's Catherine in there,' Francis told himself. 'Catherine. That's her coffin. That's where she's going to be for ever.' The vicar's voice stopped and so did his own. Adele and his father, either side of him, bowed their heads and he imitated them, staring into the grave. For no reason a bobble of mud broke off its brown wall and bumped on to the coffin lid.

Adele sighed and the semi-circle began to dissolve. The vicar was shaking the brigadier's hand; he might have been congratulating him.

'Are you all right, darling?' Adele blinked up at him from under her broad hat. She was wiping her nose with a man's hanky.

'Yes, thanks,' Francis said vaguely. 'You?'

'Oh, you know. Is my face all right?'

'Your face?'

'My mascara.'

'Oh sorry. I see.' Francis ducked under the rim of her hat. Her nostrils looked sore.

'Poor Catherine,' she sighed on him. 'Poor, poor darling. What are we to do?' She took a long breath and widened her eyes, Francis thought she was going to scream.

Then Mrs Vaisey darted between them. 'Wonderful service,' she prattled. 'Wonderful lot of people. You must be very proud of your sister. I feel quite overcome.' She wheeled away, pressing down her hat, searching for someone else she knew.

'Dear old Granny,' Adele gurgled. Her panic had gone, and she gripped Francis by the arm. 'Will you come back to the house with us, darling?'

'Well . . .'

'Please.'

'Well, honestly, I think I'd better go with Dad. I came with him and you know . . . I think I ought.'

Adele tucked her handbag hard into her armpit, biting her lip.

Francis persevered. 'He's got no one else to go back with him. You've got Granny.'

'That's not all I've got, as it happens,' she miaowed.

'What do you mean?'

'It's a surprise. He's here somewhere.' She tweaked the bag open and took out the hanky. 'You'll see.'

'Actually you have got some mascara on your face,' Francis said. 'There.' He laid his forefinger lightly on her cheekbone.

'Ow,' Adele pouted.

'I hardly touched you.'

The mark of his finger faded from Adele's face and Francis thought: she does look beautiful.

'Well, I'll see you at home then, darling,' she said airily. 'I'll go and find Granny. And your surprise.' She rustled away. It might have been the loose lining of her coat, but it sounded coarser than that. More like stockings rubbing together.

The brigadier loomed beside him. 'Mother off then?'

'She's going home; back to the house.'

A face like a bulldog approached from the crowd. 'I'm most terribly sorry about this, Edmund,' it said. 'Terrible business. Terrible.'

'Thank you.' The brigadier waved one hand backwards and forwards. 'You know my boy Francis, don't you?' They moved towards the lych-gate. The path was choked, and several people had squeezed on to the grass and were picking their way among the graves, lifting their feet up quickly as though the ground were hot.

'I'll catch you up,' said Francis, too softly for anyone to hear. He stood on the duckboards, where the coffin had waited, and gazed down. There was the spray of fine dry earth. On a face it would have looked like a birthmark. On the pale wood it was like a disease. For the first time he could clearly imagine Catherine inside the coffin. He saw her faded red hair, flicked back from her face; the little lavender veins in her eyelids; the bruised eye-sockets; her mouth sagging away from her teeth so that she seemed to be smiling; the rusty freckles across her nose. He thought he could hear the minute creak of her nails growing.

A shadow hardened at his side and he looked round.

'Jesus. Keith.'

'Hallo, Frank.' Keith was holding out his hand; he was wearing a thick black coat Francis had never seen before.

'What are you doing here?'

'I came to the funeral.' The voice was deep and confiding, like a doctor's.

'I can see that,' Francis said. Keith's hair had grown long during the summer and framed his face with dark glossy licks. He seemed older; his olive face leaner. There was a grain of stubble on his cheek. 'How did you get here?'

'Your mother.' Keith's wide mouth eased into a smile.

'What do you mean, my mother?'

'I came with her. We drove up together.' Keith paused. 'And your grandmother.'

'But how? I mean, how did you know?'

'I'd seen it in the paper,' Keith said reasonably. 'So I rang Adele and asked for a lift. I thought: why not?'

Francis looked into the grave again. Catherine had gone. 'I was just saying goodbye, you know,' he mumbled.

'What?'

'I said it's time we were going.'

Keith stepped forward, bending stiffly at the waist, taking care not to fall in. In a hard clear voice he said: 'Goodbye, dear Catherine.'

Francis swung away, slipping on a patch of flattened mud and flinging out one arm for balance.

Keith gripped him by the elbow. 'Steady there.'

Francis shook him off; his face itched.

They passed the door to the vestry and two men stepped out wearing green caps and heavy gumboots; both had spades over their shoulders like guns. 'Afternoon,' said the elder man, tipping his cap. 'Anyone else there now?'

'No. We're the last,' said Keith.

'That's right,' Francis echoed. Now he was close to the men, he could see they were father and son.

'We'll be getting on then,' said the father. 'Don't want to miss the day.' They ambled past, their heels striking the hard path with a hollow wobbling sound.

'Perhaps I'll just go and watch them,' said Keith officiously.

'Why?'

'Just to see it's done properly.'

Francis looked beyond the lych-gate at the dark coats getting into their cars. His heart skimmed inside him and his mouth was loose, as though he had no muscles in his face. 'I know you're only trying to help,' he said dully, 'but give it a rest, will you? We can manage.' His voice was so loud he thought everyone in the field ahead must be able to hear him. 'OK?' he added more gently, then walked on.

'Sure,' Keith said behind him, flatly, then again, 'Sure,' and overtook him, striding briskly up the cement track. His sleek hair flounced on his collar.

'I'll see you at the house,' Francis called after him. 'I'll introduce you to people.'

Keith gave no sign that he had heard.

They reversed into the village street. On either side people were unlocking doors, throwing coats on to back seats, lighting cigarettes.

'Look at that bloody fool,' the brigadier burst out. One of the congregation had parked across the entrance to a bunga-low, and the bungalow's owner, trying to squeeze out in his own car, had tangled front bumpers. 'Bloody fool,' said the brigadier again. 'Sorry, Francis, what were you saying? A friend?'

'Yes; just turned up.' Francis changed tack. 'Adele seemed to cope. Though how she manages with Granny, I can't think.'

'She's breaking up very fast, isn't she? Absolutely barmy, calling you Catherine like that.'

The Daimler slid into the dark garage and they squeezed out, slamming their doors. 'Oh Christ, there's thingy,' said the brigadier, stooping towards the drive. 'I'd better go and have a word.'

Francis followed him into the daylight, and the drive suddenly widened and tilted. He stretched out a hand to save himself when he fell. But he didn't fall. The drive steadied. It wasn't really wide at all. Just large enough to turn a car. In fact, here was a car now, turning and stopping outside the front door. Adele's Mini. The passenger door swung open and Granny V appeared. She was gripping her brown hat in her teeth as though she had just killed it. Her short white hair straggled like a terrier's.

Keith, who had been driving the car, laid his arm expansively along the passenger seat and spoke to Adele in the back. He had taken off his overcoat, and was flushed. He glanced up at Francis, said something and laughed. Adele turned and lifted her hat from the seat beside her, waggling it at him. Her head with her hair scraped up looked scalped.

The car rocked as Keith climbed out. He kept his back to Francis and bent through the open door, reaching in. The jacket of his suit rode up, its pert vent opening. Then the jacket slid down and Keith was turning round, holding Adele by the elbow. He dabbed a gleaming lock back from his face and smiled like a conjurer introducing a woman he had just sawn in half.

'Be an angel.' Jamie was kneeling on the floor of his study, trying to heave open his tuck-box. His right arm was in plaster; his long, loose-jointed body looked like a collapsed puppet.

Francis hoiked up the lid. 'What on earth are you doing?'

'Well,' Jamie's head disappeared and his voice was muffled, 'by my calculation it's exactly one minute past six, and it's your first evening back, and we haven't seen each other for . . .' He sat back on his heels, flaring his wide nostrils. 'So I thought we'd get drunk.' He was gripping a bottle of vodka by the neck. 'All right?'

Francis remembered Adele – 'Jamie? Is he the one with the nancy voice?' – and grinned. 'Do you want the Thames Valley Police to join in too, or are you just shouting for effect?'

'Was I shouting?'

'Pour the bloody thing out.'

'All right, all right,' Jamie drawled. 'It's Saturday – no one'll come in. It's not like Rex's over here, you know. Another country. Another set of laws.' He tapped the side of his bony nose, then unfolded upright. His dark suit was too small, and pinched him under the arms. He tipped the vodka into two white-china mugs, raising one to Francis. 'Get this down you.'

Francis lowered himself on to Jamie's desk chair. A thin metal stem supporting a small lozenge curled from below the lime-green seat.

'It's quite safe. You won't feel a thing.'

'It moves.'

Jamie groaned. 'It's on wheels, sweetheart.' He sank on to

the windowseat, rolling his eyes. He'd been to Tunisia during the summer and had his hair cut since coming back. There was a sickly white band round his head, below his dark hairline.

'You look . . .' Francis began.

'I look ghastly.' Jamie clonked his brow with his plaster. 'My father dragged me off to some appalling black magician in Dover Street. I sat there surrounded by cases full of sponges, feeling like Hans Hass, then after half an hour I found I'd been turned into the young Kenneth Williams.'

'You do look rather like him.'

'Don't think I don't know. The shame.' Jamie flexed his nostrils. 'And as for my bloody arm – that's the last time you'll catch me running down a sand-dune.'

'Yeah. I saw Alex before I came over; he filled me in.'

'Charming,' Jamie cooed.

Francis was suddenly awkward. 'I only saw him for a moment, that's all – I didn't get much. Mainly that he and his band have got an audition, or whatever you call it. Because of those fucking tapes he keeps sending off.'

Jamie swallowed, spluttering. 'Jesus wept, don't tell me he's going to make it. Quick, give me some *good* news.'

'No bombs, I gather.' Francis fidgeted in his chair.

Jamie narrowed his eyes. 'I can do better than that.'

'What? What do you know?'

'That would be telling, wouldn't it?'

'Well, tell me then, you bastard. You're obviously dying to.'

Jamie tapped the side of his nose again. 'Gower.'

'Gower? The scrubber Gower? Christ, Jamie . . .'

Jamie put on his shocked voice. 'I don't know why you're being so moral about this.'

'I'm not being moral. It's just that I'm not supposed to know about the bombs, and neither are you.' Francis glanced out of the window; the heads and shoulders of two boys bobbed past.

'Do I detect the note of authority there?'

'No, of course not,' said Francis. 'I just mean bombs are bombs, that's all.' He twirled out of his chair and spun in a full circle. The walls of the little room were covered with dark-red shiny wrapping-paper; the only picture, a print of Pushkin in a gold frame, hung above the desk. 'It feels nice, your place. It's always the same.'

'I achieved perfection early,' said Jamie.

Francis stood up, kissed his hair, then quickly sat down again.

'What's that for?'

'Being here.'

Jamie stretched out with his injured arm behind his head. 'Your Mister Roberts told me your Mister Ogilvie turned up,' he said.

'At the funeral, you mean?' Francis sighed. 'Yes, he did. With my mother. He asked her to take him. He got his come-uppance in a way; he had to travel with my granny, and she's insane. At the party thing after the funeral she kept telling everyone he was my mother's new husband. It was hilarious.'

'Sounds it,' Jamie said flatly. 'Your old man must have loved it.'

'Who knows what he thinks?' Francis said. 'He never uttered. He never does. In an odd sort of way the whole thing seemed to perk him up; the funeral and everything.'

'What'll he do now?'

'God knows. Whatever it is, I'll only find out when it's happened.' Francis gulped his drink. 'Can I have some more?' He stood up and the red paper rustled at him.

'Fill me up too, Scottie.' Jamie held out his own mug. 'Get back to Ogilvie. I thought he was your friend.'

'He is my friend.' Francis sat down cautiously, but his chair still scuttled backwards. His face was hot. 'You won't tell anyone, will you?'

'What?'

'What I'm about to tell you.'

'Depends how interesting it is. If it's that Middleton's

got terminal clap, or something like that, I'll tell everyone. I'll write to the papers.'

'Be serious, you winnet.'

'I'm deadly serious.'

'No, *serious* serious.' Francis squinted into a pigeon-hole in Jamie's desk. It was stacked with postcards, the top one showing a photograph of Mahler. He was standing in profile, hands on hips in a grey suit, squinting a little through his pince-nez. His hair was thrust carelessly back from his high forehead.

'What's that?' Jamie asked anxiously, hoisting himself on to one elbow.

'Your picture of the great Gustav,' Francis said. His tongue felt heavy. 'I was just thinking: I suppose that's what you want to look like.'

Jamie relaxed. 'Only when my Kenneth Williams years are over. Anyway, I don't want glasses. Now; will you please stay on the point?'

Francis cleared his throat. 'Keith wrote to Catherine before she died,' he said. It sounded ridiculous.

Jamie chuckled. 'It's hardly a crime, you know, darling. I mean – girls: they make boys write to them and things.'

Francis stared at the heavy cream window-frame behind Jamie's head. 'What I'm trying to explain is very difficult,' he said laboriously. 'It's that Keith wrote to Catherine but somehow it left me out.'

Jamie sucked in his cheeks. If I were anyone else, Francis thought, he'd tell me to fuck off; 'I'm sorry,' he said. 'I can't explain what I mean.'

'No; it's all right.' Jamie was suddenly businesslike, sitting upright and speaking briskly. 'I think what you're saying is perfectly simple. You're saying that Ogilvie, who had been keen on you, got keen on your sister. Am I right?'

'Well, yes – but it's more than that. There was something about it all which made me feel he'd never been my friend. Never.' Francis took a big swallow from his mug, then added, 'Jesus, I wish I'd never started this.'

'No, I'm getting interested.' Jamie leant forward. 'But why do you think he was spending all that time with you? All that sloping off to the wood and the lake and everything?'

'I think I was a means to an end.'

'Disgusting expression. Did you have a lot of sex?'

'I don't know.' Francis felt helpless. 'What's a lot?'

'A lot is more than once a day. Quite a lot is only once a day.'

'Quite a lot, then,' Francis said slowly; his tongue was unwieldy in his mouth. 'But usually more than once in that once, if you see what I mean.'

Jamie held up one hand. 'Please. I'm only trying to get the general picture, not a blow-by-blow.'

'There's another thing.' Francis hesitated. 'I think he's trying something with my mother.'

Jamie gave a high, incredulous laugh. 'Jesus Christ, F, you are in a bad way. I mean I'm sorry, but . . . Hang on.' He drained his mug. 'Here – fill me up – I'm sorry, but really . . .'

Francis tilted the bottle; it was warm and slippery. 'I suppose it does sound a bit silly, doesn't it?' He wiped his hands on his trousers and stared out of the window. Zigzag brick-patterns danced on the chapel wall opposite.

'No, not silly, exactly.' Jamie was straight-faced again. 'Are you saying he's been to bed with her, or what?'

'There was just something about the way they were together. I don't know. Seeing them in the car together made me . . .' He left the sentence unfinished. He was suddenly bored; he couldn't see why he was bothering.

A breath of wind slithered across the windowsill, and a white sliver swayed in the polish on his shoes. Mrs Banyard had handed them to him in the scullery that morning. 'I've just done them quickly for you,' she said. Then she had stood on the front doorstep, waving as the taxi took him away to the station. He saw his father too, puce in the chilly wind, holding up one hand like a child, opening and closing his fingers.

Jamie was in front of him, resting one hand on his shoulder. 'It's all right, you know,' he said softly.

'Your plaster feels heavy.' Francis sank forward, leaning his head on Jamie's chest. 'Oh shit,' he said, 'don't you go all soft and sorry for me, I'm counting on you.'

Jamie buried his face in Francis' hair. 'You smell clean.'

'I am clean.'

'Not for long, I hope.'

Francis gave a wet chuckle; his neck began to ache.

'Since you've told me your secret,' Jamie mumbled. 'I'll tell you mine. You know I said I bust my arm falling down a sand-dune? Well, I didn't. I fell off the side of the bath.'

Francis jerked his head up and Jamie stepped back, standing on one leg and biting his lower lip.

'Oh, no,' Francis wailed. 'Surely not doing *that*. How, for Christ's sake?'

'Pre-bath job, bigger number than I thought, weak grip on enamel, slip off, keen not to bonk whanger on lino, awkward landing, bingo. Arm broken.'

Francis beamed. 'Have you had to go and see Sister Limm?'

'God yes,' Jamie said keenly. 'First day back.'

'Any sign of the hot spoon?'

Jamie paced to and fro across the narrow study, his plaster tucked inside his jacket. 'Napoleon he say: No, no sign of the hot spoon.' He turned to Francis. 'But you know, it's funny you should mention it. I used to think the whole hot spoon thing was a load of bollocks, then just at the end of last term I had a little run-in with Savoury – you know Savoury?'

'Urgh.'

'Yes, quite. Mind gamma, but A1 packed lunch – absolutely vast. Anyway, he said he'd had some sort of throat bug and I said not surprising and he said he'd gone down to the infirmary and seen Sister L, and she'd had his trousers off in no time. You know what the old bat's like. Cough and drop, the works. So, while she was fiddling around he started to crank up, and she gave him a look, opened the drawer cool as a cucumber, produced this spoon, and banged him on the end of the willy with it.'

'Ouch.'

'Just like someone attacking a boiled egg, Savoury said.'

'Jesus. And?'

'And he cranked down again pretty smartish.' Jamie paused, long-faced and intent. 'But the really interesting thing – or the thing which struck me, anyway – is that before biffing him, she actually did run the bloody spoon under a hot tap. Can you believe it? I mean, I'd have thought if she really wanted to put a chap off, it'd have been a *cold* tap.'

'It must be some longing for cleanliness,' Francis said seriously.

'Amazing.'

'Religious.'

'Next to godliness.' Jamie sighed and shook his head. Then he held out his hand to Francis. 'Now you've laughed, you can go.'

Francis stood up and kissed him on the cheek. 'I don't believe a bloody word you've said, of course.'

Jamie stared at him gravely. 'Just go, will you?'

Francis took a packet of Polos from his coat pocket, and slipped one into Jamie's mouth, one into his own.

'Go.' Jamie pointed towards the door with his white, heavy arm.

'Hey! Where are you off to?'

The brick rocket of the clock-tower reared out of the twilight ahead of Francis; sparrows were fussing in a large bay bush away to his right. He turned and saw Middleton rasping towards him.

'Back to Rex's.' He sucked his Polo and it shattered.

'Oh, it's you, Mayne. I didn't see.' Middleton's crinkled hair gleamed like a corn dolly; his gown was neatly folded across his shoulder. 'I didn't know you were back. I'm sorry about your business. Terrible.'

'Yes, I came back this afternoon. I've been seeing Jamieson.' Francis was expressionless. 'We were comparing notes on our new responsibilities.'

Middleton stared at him blankly. 'Which way are you walking?'

'Oh, just up by chapel and round. Back to my study.'

'I'll walk with you.' Middleton's coat flapped open and brass buttons winked on his waistcoat.

'Nice waistcoat,' said Francis, 'if I may say so.'

Middleton squinted down. 'Oh, do you think so? Thanks. Might as well use our privileges to the hilt, I think.'

'Absolutely to the hilt.'

Middleton's square jaw tightened. Francis thought: he looks the kind of brainless sod you see in war films, about to walk into a minefield. He imagined him cartwheeling through a saffron sky, the gown flying off his shoulder like a vulture lumbering off a perch.

'Did you?' Francis asked.

'What's that?'

'Have a good holiday.'

'Wonderful. Algarve.' They entered the shadow of the clock-tower; long glowing windows in the chapel beside them showed an obscure pageant of dark-blue figures.

'Someone's in chapel,' Francis said futilely.

'Shouldn't be. Not at this time.'

Francis glanced over his shoulder across the deserted quadrangle and saw a sparrow fly out of the big bay bush. Then there was a scratching rustle and a sharp crack, like two pieces of wood banged together. Immediately, a bright yellow flag of flame waved out of the top, shrank back, and flapped sideways. The bush began to burn fiercely.

'Good God!' Middleton farted and flung one arm across his face. 'What the hell's that?'

'It's a bomb, I think.'

'Good God.'

'It's set fire to that bush.'

'Good God.'

A sparrow whizzed overhead like a stone. Somewhere a door slammed and a voice yodelled 'Whoopsadaisy!'

Middleton was leaping from foot to foot. 'It's OK, Mayne,' he shouted. 'I'll handle this. You stay here. Clear the area. I'll deal with this.'

'OK.' Francis paused, then said gently, 'We have forgot the fart.'

'The little *buggers*,' shouted Middleton. 'What?'

'We have forgot the fart.'

'What the hell are you talking about, Mayne?' Middleton pounded off, snatching his gown from his shoulder.

Boys began to appear at once, some creeping cautiously, a few racing and shouting. Francis watched their silhouettes against the flames and remembered a drawing he had once seen of Robinson Crusoe concealed in a palm tree, staring at savages dancing round a fire on a beach.

He turned into the small quadrangle below King's Tower and looked up at the uncurtained window of Keith's study. He imagined him working – coat off, shirt sleeves rolled up, frowning at the voices below – and turned away into the covered corridor.

A few boys tore past him, but he didn't know any of them. Everyone was absorbed in their own business. When he reached the double doors to the chapel he knew no one was watching. He twisted the heavy iron handle. There was a click, then its skittering echo. He heaved the door shut behind him. This time the echo was a deep booming ricochet.

He stepped under the screen. The steep valley of pews was lit by a few spots high on the bare walls, and the black and white squares of the floor shone like ice.

'Is anyone there?' His voice mellowed as it soared into the enormous roof.

There was a creak and he walked towards it, wide-eyed. 'Is anyone there?' he said again. He felt absurd. Why was he there himself? He hadn't meant to be.

A terse hiss reached him, then a whisper: 'No. You,' and

a few hollow clumps. A fair-haired boy rose out of a pew, waddled to its end and traipsed down a short flight of steps into the aisle. It was Tavenot.

'Sorry, Mayne. I didn't hear you. I didn't know anyone was here.' Tavenot stared Francis in the chest. His lips shone.

'Don't you mean we?'

'Sorry?'

'Don't you mean *we* didn't hear you?'

'Oh, you mean Ventnor.' Tavenot jerked his head sideways.

'Do I?'

'Yes. Ventnor and I were just talking. Ventnor's a sacristan now. I'm chief sacristan – perhaps you knew?' Tavenot pushed a handful of limp yellow curls back from his forehead.

'No, I didn't. I've only just got back.'

'I heard you were getting back late,' said Tavenot smarmily. 'I'm very sorry, Mayne.'

'What about?'

'Your sister. Jamieson told me.'

Francis hesitated. 'You know Jamieson well?'

Tavenot's eyes narrowed. 'We're both members of the Victorian Society.'

'I see.' Francis glanced towards the dark pews. 'Don't you think we might meet Ventnor? He must be getting lonely in there.'

Tavenot called out. 'Tom? Mayne wants to meet you. He says will you please come down.'

There was a second small barrage of thumps, and a dark boy emerged, his head drooping as though he'd been hanged.

'Ventnor?'

'Yes, Mayne,' said the sulky head. It had a double crown.

'You know you shouldn't be here, don't you?'

'It's all right. I'm signed out.' Ventnor glanced up; he had the dry, rosy cheeks of a farmer's boy.

'I was telling him a sacristan's duties,' said Tavenot.

'Really? Do you think you're going to enjoy them?'

'It's very interesting work,' said Tavenot. 'But I think we'd better be getting along now. We'd nearly finished, hadn't we, Tom?'

Between the top of Ventnor's zip and the band of his trousers a snick of white shirt was sticking out. Like a scut, Francis thought. A scut back-to-front.

'You know where the lights turn off, do you?' Tavenot asked with a little laugh. 'The chaplain goes spare when they're left on, and he'll think we did it.'

'Just go, will you?'

They bobbed down the dusky aisle. One of them – Ventnor, probably, Francis thought – had metal clips on his heels like Jamie. His footsteps chipped and rang on the black and white tiles; then came the boom of the door closing.

Francis faced the altar, silence lapping like liquid. The reredos towered above him, each level less distinct than the one beneath. Only in the big centrepiece, the crucifixion, could he make out the details of faces. Christ's was a smooth yellow egg with holes for eyes and a mouth; the huddle of mourners at the foot of the cross looked like monkeys.

He stared at the 'Flight into Egypt'. The background was a battered shield, splitting on one side into a palm tree. Lifting out of this shield towards him were Joseph and Mary and the donkey. Joseph was in profile, half-hidden under a cowl, the dull blob of his face utterly without character. Mary was striding along in her ankle-length gown, her sharp sandals stabbing out. Francis smiled. 'Where do you think you're going?' he asked aloud, then licked his finger and stuck it up her dress. It was jagged inside her, and when he withdrew his finger, it was black with dust. He rubbed it on his knee and saw the vicar at Catherine's funeral, wiping his hand on his trousers under his surplice. 'How could you?' he whispered. 'How could you?'

The chapel door clicked again, and Francis scurried down the altar steps towards the first block of pews, shuffling into the darkness until he was invisible. Heavy shoes rapped on the aisle and stopped. There was a grunting sigh. Francis held his breath and peered out. It was Middleton, kneeling rigidly in front of the altar like a figure on a tomb – his blond head tipped savagely forward, his back straight, his hands clenched and thumbs stuck out stiffly in line with the seams in his trousers. He was deep in prayer.

Keith recognized the knock and whisked open his study door. His hair was cut short, jutting in thick, stubby eaves above his ears. He kissed Francis on both cheeks. 'What kept you?'

'You wouldn't like it if I told you, but I will. Chapel.' Francis flopped into the wicker chair.

'Chapel?' Keith repeated incredulously. 'Christ.' He shut the door and sat down, lacing his fingers on the desk-top. 'It's been a long time.'

Francis didn't know where to begin. Keith felt like a stranger – he wasn't the same person that had been at Catherine's funeral. He was younger again, but not in ways Francis understood. He was full of secrets.

'I'm sorry I didn't write,' Keith was saying. 'I ought to have.'

'It's hard to know what to say.'

'It wasn't that. I wasn't *so* busy.'

'It was nice of you to come to the funeral.'

'It was a pleasure.' Keith frowned across his desk. 'No – I mean it. How's Adele, do you reckon? She seemed to be getting over it to me.'

'You've talked to her, have you?'

'I thanked her for taking me.' Keith picked up a yellow pencil and rolled it between his palms; it made a dry thrumming.

Francis didn't have time to think. 'But you did write to Catherine,' he said.

'It was easier to write to her somehow,' Keith said smoothly. 'Probably because I didn't know her so well. I didn't feel I had to go through things. I wrote to cheer her up, really. Does that upset you?'

Francis felt lost. 'Sorry?'

'Does it upset you that I didn't write to you?'

Francis saw the ragged edge of Keith's letter sticking out of the books by Catherine's bed. 'I didn't follow what you said a minute ago,' he said.

'What was that?' Keith had crouched beside his desk and switched on the kettle. His face was flushed and solicitous when he sat up again. 'I thought we might have some coffee.'

'I said,' Francis whispered, 'I can't seem to get over it.'

Keith spread his fingers on his desk and began speaking confidently. 'Listen, Frank. You've been through things which are bound to make differences – I know that. I know what being at home is like, even without all you've had. You can't do what you want. I mean, Jesus. *I* feel that – in London! And my people know the score; they're decent about things.' He smiled out of the side of his mouth. 'See what I'm saying?'

Francis struggled to concentrate. 'I suppose,' he said wearily. 'Everyone keeps giving me advice. I think I'll just save it up and think about it later.'

'What's that supposed to mean?'

'I wish someone would tell me something as simple as what I feel.'

'Is what I said difficult? I didn't realize. Anyway, what do you mean, everyone?'

'You.' Francis shrugged. 'Jamie.'

'Jamieson?' Keith pounced. 'When?'

'Earlier this evening.' Francis rubbed his forehead. 'I think I must've lost my brain.' Steam was clouding from the kettle. 'Shouldn't you do something about that?'

Keith sat on his haunches, made Francis a mug of coffee and passed it up to him. 'What I'm telling you,' he said, smiling, 'is that you've got to *do* something. Is that simple enough?'

Francis blew on his coffee. 'I'm sorry, Keith.'

'Oh don't start your apologizing already, Frank. You've only just got here.' He sat at his desk again and said eagerly,

'Listen. Let me try something on you. At the end of October there's a big Vietnam rally due for Hyde Park – like the one in March, only bigger.'

'How do you know about it?'

'Everyone knows about it. My Dad's partner, in his practice, he's got a son at Manchester who told me about it. He's going.'

Francis took a sip of coffee. 'They'll never let us,' he said ploddingly.

'They'll never know! We'll tell them we're going to the Natural History Museum or something.'

'But what about your work?'

'To hell with work. It's only a day – there's no big deal.'

'What's his name, this Manchester person?'

'Bos. It's short for Boswell. His father's mad on Dr Johnson. What do you think?'

'I don't know.'

'Why are you being so cautious, Frank? It's not like you.'

'No, well, like you said, there are differences.' Francis put down his coffee; he hadn't asked any of the things he had wanted to ask, and now it was too late. Keith had hurried him away from them all, and he had offered no resistance.

'You're not being chicken, are you?' Keith's wide mouth curled.

'No, of course not,' Francis stumbled. 'I just don't see what it's got to do with me.'

'Why should it have something to do with you?'

Francis shrugged.

'Great. So it's fixed then.' Keith stood up. 'Now.' He put his hands on his hips. 'What's next?'

Francis lifted one hand like a woman offering her fingers to be kissed. 'Help me up,' he said. 'I'm whacked.'

'It's normal,' Keith answered. 'I told you before.'

'I remember. It feels a long time ago, doesn't it?'

Keith slowly closed and opened his eyes, then whispered, 'Will you stay, or is that a difference too?'

Francis swallowed. Somewhere in the building below them

a voice was calling goodnight to other voices, its brisk yap softening as it rose through the smooth floors. 'Yes, all right,' he heard himself say, 'I'll stay for a bit. I'd like that.'

After a few days no one mentioned Catherine any more, or told Francis how sorry they were. He didn't mind. He knew if people stopped saying things it didn't always mean they stopped feeling them. When he looked across his study and found Alex smiling at him he was sure he knew why.

But as the days milled past he lost confidence. Perhaps Catherine had just been forgotten? If she had, it meant he was ordinary again, and vulnerable. He invented new ways of keeping her alive. He took up cross-country running. Every day after lunch he put on his regulation blue shorts and white singlet, and toiled off across the playing fields into the wood. Occasionally Catherine's face erupted out of the bracken at his feet. He tracked it in a large painful circle, pounding out of the wood over a few thistly fields, then back through the village and up the drive into King's Tower.

Except when he was running, Catherine seldom appeared in daylight. There were too many people; too many things to do. At night she always returned, while boys fidgeted indifferently in the cubicles round him. It became a ritual for him to press his face into the pillow, let red streaks and blotches invade the blackness, then find her patient face: pastry-skinned, her freckles rusting.

The evening before he went to London with Keith, he kept her waiting. It was late, but he wanted to ask something about the magazine. He floated up the cold steps of the tower.

'Yeah, I know, but it's two months now. And I mean all he does is get weirder and weirder.' It was Keith's deep voice, coming from the bathroom at the turn in the stairs below his study. Francis froze as if a searchlight had settled on him; he imagined the big metal baths facing each other behind the closed door, and the slippery bodies in them like seals. He saw the long duckboard on the lead floor, submerged in tropical water.

'I knew her too, you know,' Keith went on, aggrieved.

'Yes, but she was his sister, you tool.' That was Alex. 'She wasn't your sister.' There was a swirl of water; Alex must have reached for a sponge.

Then a third voice broke in, Savoury's. 'You didn't know her well though, did you?' it said derisively. 'I mean, you never poked her or anything, did you?'

Francis heard the blood surge round his body and sizzle into his ears. Surely they would hear it too, and stop? He couldn't just burst in – they'd know he'd been listening. It would be so shaming.

'Must you always be so fucking gross, Savoury?' That was Alex again.

'I'm just saying . . .'

'That's typical patronizing shit, Savoury,' said Keith. 'It's the only thing you upper-class wankers can think about. Poke. Possess. You make me puke.'

There was a hot silence, then Savoury again, wheedling. 'Fighting a bit dirty aren't we, Ogilvie? A minute ago you were calling him weird, now you're standing up for him. I think you're just jealous of him seeing anyone. Jamieson.' He snorted. 'God.'

'Jealous of God? Don't be an arsehole.'

'You should know if I'm an arsehole; you see enough of them.'

A heavy slick of water flopped on to the floor and Alex shouted, 'Fuck off, both of you. Both of you. What's got into you, for Christ's sake?' Francis realized his skin was damp – a mizzle coating his forehead. He licked his lips.

'Well,' Alex continued reasonably, 'I must say I haven't noticed him being so different. Not in the study, anyway. Quieter, but not what you said, Keith. Just working a lot. Doing the magazine.'

'Doing the magazine!' Keith exclaimed. 'Every time he wants to do something for the magazine he comes and asks me.'

Sweat squeezed into the corner of Francis' eye. Now nothing about him was making any noise; his heart was silent, his blood sluggish.

'*Asks* you?' said Savoury. 'Is that what you do? *Ask* each other things?'

'Oh fuck,' Keith snapped. 'Actually seriously fuck. That's it. I've had enough.' There was a sucking crash and wet smacking on the duckboard. Francis imagined the water streaming off Keith's dark legs, then looked at his shoes and saw them treading back down the stairs, turning round and climbing up again. His head was airy and vacant, cold at the back where he'd been leaning against the wall of the stair-well.

He rattled the door open. Keith was hunched in his bath with water brimming round his ears; his wet hair was swept back. So it hadn't been him that had got out. Alex was stooped above him, a white towel tied round his waist. He looked enormous; his thick muscular body shone. Savoury was lolling in a fawn dressing-gown against the far wall.

'Close the door, old man,' Savoury said slowly. 'You're letting all the heat out.'

Francis groped behind him and pulled the door shut.

'Jesus,' said Alex, straightening. Keith slid up against the end of the bath, squirting a little jet of dirty water out of his mouth. 'Hi,' he said softly. 'This bastard here was trying to drown me.'

'Yes, I heard a racket,' said Francis.

'Not from too far away I hope,' Alex asked with a dry laugh. 'Don't want Rex bursting in.'

Shame, Francis remembered: I felt ashamed. That's why I'm standing here like this. 'Oh no,' he said, smiling. 'Not from far away.'

'Keith was saying I couldn't sing,' Alex laughed again. 'So I thought I'd drown him.'

'Yes.' Francis wished he could think of something that would make them feel easy, and stop the silence crackling.

Eventually Savoury shouldered away from the wall. 'I'm going to bed,' he said, and left without anyone saying good-night.

Alex struggled into his dressing-gown, unhooked his towel and buffeted his tangled curly hair. 'Savoury really is an unspeakable shit,' he mumbled.

'Really a little *shit*,' said Keith. 'If he doesn't watch himself . . . But of course he'll be fine. Scum like that always float to the top.'

Francis stared at his glossy seal's head lipping the water. All it needed was both hands and a long shunt down, and he'd disappear.

Alex emerged from his towel. 'I think I'll turn in too if you don't mind. I want to be at my best for tomorrow.'

'Chedworth sodding Villa,' said Keith. 'Whatever possessed you?'

Alex brightened. 'My passionate interest in sites of major archaeological significance with smoking facilities.' He rattled open the door. 'Goodnight.'

Francis meant to answer but the door shut before he could speak. He sat on the edge of the empty bath opposite Keith; he felt exhausted.

Keith wriggled loosely. 'Do you want to get in?' The water slithered off his shoulders. The black smudge of hair in the centre of his chest was like a paw-print.

Francis shook his head. 'Not if you don't mind,' he said hollowly.

'Why should I mind?'

'I thought you might want me to.'

'Well, I do. But I understand.' The cloudy water lapped at his nipples and the thin hair wavered like seaweed on pebbles. 'What are you thinking?' he went on coaxingly.

Francis said the first thing that came into his head. 'About tomorrow.'

'It'll be just what you need,' Keith told him. 'A famous

day.' His broad mouth stretched without showing his teeth. 'You are glad we're going, aren't you?'

'It's all fixed now, isn't it?'

'I'm so glad.' Keith heaved himself to his feet, and the white walls glistened – the paint was blistered and looked as though it might pop open in shining sores at any moment.

'Frank?' Keith's voice was remote; he had tied a towel round his waist and steam was curling from his chest and shoulders. Very slowly, he scooped a tablet of soap off the rim of the bath, squeezed it and replaced it. Then he dipped his hand in the sinking water, withdrew it, twitched the towel open, and languidly pulled his cock. 'Frank?' Keith whispered again.

Francis shook his head. 'It's very nice of you, but no thank you.' It sounded as though he were refusing a scone.

The damp air swilled between them.

'Is that it then?' Keith seemed to be repeating something he'd learnt in a book. His cock bobbed downwards and pointed at the duckboard. Francis smeared his hand over his forehead and said: 'I don't know; I can't think.'

'It's me, isn't it?' said Keith eagerly.

Francis stood up. He didn't mean to touch Keith, but realized he must have done when he saw him sit down smartly on the bath. 'I'm sorry, really I am. I just can't think.' He slid the door open and shut and reeled in the darkness.

The floorboards creaked and a ghost in blue pyjamas appeared, fair hair rumpled, knuckling one eye.

'Fox?' Francis asked. He sensed Keith's silence behind him.

'Yes, sir.'

'I'm not sir.'

'No, Mayne.'

'What are you doing?'

'Going to the toilet.'

'To the lavatory.'

'Yes.'

'All right, then. Goodnight.'

114

'Goodnight, sir.' The little figure meandered away, still rubbing one eye. Francis wanted to call him back, to wrap him in his arms and snuff up his sweet sleepy fug. He watched him turn the corner and heard the lavatory door closing. Then there was the slap of a footstep in the bathroom and he turned towards the stairs.

On the train to London Francis told Keith about his dream.

'I was walking along this river bank.'

'Oh yeah?' They were side by side, facing the engine. Keith had taken the corner seat and was watching the Thames Valley unreel. 'We all know about water and dreams.'

'Yes, well. There was this river bank, and this dirty water, and I dived in.'

'Oh yeah?'

'Yes,' Francis persevered. 'But it wasn't wet, and I swam down to the bed of the river – I could breathe all right – and I found this sort of trap-door thing which I opened.'

Keith hunched sullenly against the window. They were wearing their dark suits and overcoats, and both had taken off their ties. Keith had twitched the hair out from behind his ears so they were almost hidden. He looks tired, Francis thought; he hasn't slept.

'And under the trap-door was this huge cathedral made of iron – iron columns everywhere – and it was full of water, too, but I could still breathe, and I sort of drifted down to the floor of the cathedral and there you were.'

'Stark naked, I hope.'

Francis smiled uncertainly. 'Anyway, I went up to you to talk but you just smiled at me and . . .'

'What's the matter?'

'Well, now I'm telling you about it I see what it means.'

'You expect me to believe that?' Keith said sourly. 'That you only see now? How naïve do you think I am?'

'No, really, I . . .'

'Tell me then. I want to make sure you've got it right.'

115

Francis opened his right hand and stared at his palm. 'You just smiled and that was it,' he continued dully. 'And I floated back up through the cathedral then up through the river and on to the bank.'

'Free?'

'I knew you were still there.'

Keith looked out of the window and his jaw hardened. 'Mister fucking polite as per. Still, you wouldn't talk last night, so I suppose I ought to be grateful to hear something today. Even something so roundabout as this.'

'Oh,' Francis said hopelessly. He wondered whether Keith was going to hit him, and his stomach stirred as if it were a tangle of live wires.

'Well, we're both free, aren't we?' Keith said. The river bulged towards their window, bringing close a boy in a yellow anorak fishing from a pier; he was swinging his head as he tried to focus on faces in the carriage windows. Keith took a deep breath. 'But here we are,' he went on airily. 'Here we are.' He ran his hand through his hair and turned decisively. 'Frank, there's something I haven't told you.'

Francis felt nothing was in his control any more. 'Yes?' he said vaguely.

'Not about yesterday; about today. I think we shouldn't talk about yesterday any more.' Keith's voice was thin and rapid – quite unlike the voice he'd just been using. 'You might think it's a bit daft – I do a bit – but Bos says it'll work. When we get to Hyde Park, if it gets nasty like it was supposed to last time, we'll need to look after ourselves.'

'What do you mean? Fighting?'

'The police and things. Bos says if we have any trouble with them we'll have to freak out their horses.'

Francis was relieved. 'I know about horses.'

'Not about police horses you don't.'

'I do. I read about it. You throw marbles under their hooves.'

Keith lowered his voice. 'This is something better; something that really makes them go bananas.'

There was a thunderous clanking as they rushed over an

iron bridge; Francis let it fade then asked, 'What's that, then?'

'Lion's dung,' Keith said.

'*Lion's dung?*'

'You throw it in front of their horses and they completely freak out.'

Francis chuckled. 'Don't be ridiculous.'

'I'm not. It's been tried and it really works.'

'Who says?'

'Bos says.'

'Jesus, Keith. Has he seen it work?'

'Don't Jesus Keith me,' Keith said angrily. 'Of course he has. I told you it sounded a bit daft.'

Francis crossed his legs. 'I don't believe this. Lion's dung.'

'Don't keep saying it. Bos says it works and he's bringing some with him.'

'Where'd he get it? A health-food shop?'

'The zoo, arsehole. Manchester Zoo.'

'Bribe a keeper, did he?'

'Fuck off, Frank.' Keith's face was flushed. 'It's important, this. It's a serious demo. We don't know what's going to happen.'

'Well, we know one thing. The Manchester and Oxford-shire Dung-sprinklers will be giving their London première. Vietnam Charity Dung Sprinkle.'

The ghost of Keith's face glared from the window as they crashed through a tunnel; his mouth gaped but Francis couldn't hear what he said.

'What?'

'Nothing,' said Keith. 'Let's talk about something else.'

Francis dug in his overcoat pocket. 'Do you want a cigarette, you bastard?' he asked flatly. Keith took one and lit up without thanking him. A few moments later they pulled into Reading and their compartment filled up. They didn't speak again until they reached Paddington.

★

Keith skipped on to the platform before the train stopped. Francis imagined him stumbling on the grey asphalt, sprawling on his face with blood clogging his nose.

'Come on.' Keith beckoned with one arm and Francis jumped down beside him. Within seconds the platform was gorged with people – dark-suited men peering for a way through; a scowling, duffel-coated man who clouted Francis with his satchel and snarled, 'Move over, you rough cunt.'

Keith was breathless. 'You ain't seen nothing yet,' he said. 'You wait till we get to the demo.'

Francis smoothed his hair across his forehead. He was in a foreign city; Adele's city. These people were all utterly strange to him. He shoved past the ticket barrier and swirled towards the Underground.

'Well done, mate. Smoke?' Keith was clattering down the steps, offering a cigarette over his shoulder without looking round.

Francis put the cigarette in his mouth and touched the dry filter with the tip of his tongue. His stomach churned.

'In a bit,' he shouted, putting the cigarette in his pocket.

Keith spun away on to the escalator. In the crown of his head, where his hair flopped heavily away from a bald spot the size of a sixpence, the scalp was as white as flour. Francis wanted to put the tip of his tongue on the scalp, as he had on the filter. He looked down the dizzy descent. If he pushed now, all these people would topple forward like dolls off a shelf.

They squeezed on to a train, and when the curved door whirred shut Francis bowed his head to inhale Keith's parched lemon smell.

'Amazing, isn't it?' Keith muttered obliviously. 'All these people here all the time.' Francis said nothing and closed his eyes.

At Notting Hill the day seemed colder, the light a duller grey. Francis thought they must have travelled many miles, and emerged in a different city; he turned a full circle under a concrete overhang sheltering a row of shops. Leaning against the doorjamb of a newsagent, and only slowly straightening as Keith approached, was a tall shadow in an army trenchcoat. Brown hair almost entirely covered the face, and at first Francis took it to be a beard. Then the head shook, the hair parted, and the face emerged clean-shaven: a dwindling jaw and a pug nose straddled by wire spectacles. It looked like an Identikit picture, made up from separate pieces. Francis heard Adele's voice: 'Oh these poor people with thin hair – it's such bad luck. There's not a thing they can do with it.'

'Here,' Keith was saying. 'Frank. This is Bos. Bos, Frank.'

'Hallo.' Francis put out his hand.

'Hi,' grunted Bos. 'Can't shake, I'm afraid.' He hoisted a bulging white plastic bag.

'I hope you haven't been waiting here long.' Francis swallowed and tried roughening his voice. 'We came as quick as we could, but the crowds . . .'

'Yeah.' Bos nodded and his hair flew across his face again. 'It's the fuzz.'

'Did you travel up this morning? Down, I mean.' Francis couldn't control his voice; he grinned.

Bos gave him a surprisingly wide smile. 'Last night, so I crashed with a friend. In Portobello.' He looked at Keith and shook the plastic bag. 'I got the stuff.'

'Great.' Keith parted the lips of the bag. 'Hey great. Paaugh!' His head jerked back and he wiped his eyes. 'Hey Frank. Get a load of this.'

Francis peered at a damp, dark porridge with a few wisps of straw poking through the surface. It smelt intensely hot, like a splash of ammonia. 'Jesus,' he gasped.

Bos nodded hard. 'Yeah.'

'You collected it all right?' Keith said. 'No hassles?'

'Sure. No sweat.'

'How?' asked Francis, still prim.

'Cinch. Bribed a warder at the zoo. It was great – he had this little cap with "Big-Cat House" above the peak thing. I said I was doing biology and needed it for research.'

'And he believed you? Great,' said Keith.

'How do you know it's lion?' Francis heard himself ask.

'Of course it's lion,' said Keith.

'But it might not be. It might be hippo. Or llama.'

'What's got into you?'

'Nothing's got into me. I just wondered how Bos knew, that's all.'

Bos shuddered as though someone was walking over his grave. 'Like I said, we bribed a warder. It was a gas. He was a young guy, see, and I bribed him with bootleg tapes. Hendrix, mainly.'

'What a gas,' Keith echoed, and offered Bos a cigarette, thrusting the packet urgently towards him.

'Great,' said Bos. 'Ta.' Keith's hand keenly shielded the flame as if a strong wind had sprung up.

'Shall we go, Bos?' Francis asked. 'Isn't it time?'

Bos was laughing at something Keith had been telling him; his glasses flashed blankly.

'Yeah. Yeah, all right. All right, Keith?'

'Sure.' Keith patted Bos on the arm. 'Don't panic, Frank, we won't be late. There's loads of time.'

'Yes I know, but I thought there was a march,' said Francis. He couldn't tell whether he was angry or not. He couldn't hold his feelings in shape. 'But where does it start? It must start somewhere, then end at Hyde Park.'

'We're just going to the demo bit, not the march bit,' said Bos, tucking a strand of hair behind his ear.

'That's right,' said Keith. 'Like I said. Just to the demo.'

'I was only asking,' said Francis.

Bos pulled a purple woollen hat from an inside pocket and tugged it on to his head.

'Great hat,' said Keith, turning up the collar of his overcoat, but Bos was disappearing into the Underground and didn't hear. Keith hesitated in the entrance. 'What the fuck's eating you, Frank?' he hissed. 'Asking all those arsehole questions. If you want to come, just come.' He swooped down the dark steps.

Francis struggled to stay close on the train, but strangers kept wedging in front of him. Bos' arm hung down between a Japanese couple, their immaculate faces puckering as the bitter stench from the plastic bag enveloped them. At the third stop the arm twitched away, and Francis swam on to the platform after it. The Japanese couple were chattering and waving their delicate hands in front of their faces. He released himself to the crowd.

Keith and Bos were tucked to one side of the exit.

'OK?' Bos was clutching the plastic bag like someone bringing a present to a party.

'Great,' said Francis. He had emerged into yet another city. To right and left the wide streets were choked; every doorway, every alley and shopfront was jammed. He gave a little jump, and saw an ocean of heads undulating beneath a low mist. Higgledy-piggledy placards and banners poked up, and above them squatted the pompous block he knew was Marble Arch. Above that was the empty white sky.

There were voices. Odd, he thought, not to have noticed them before, they were so loud. They seemed to be coming from a long way away: groups chanting; single bellows; the tinny bark of a tannoy and its whine. They made him relaxed – almost sleepy. Then from the other side of Marble Arch came another chant:

> Ho, Ho, Ho Chi Minh.
> Hot chocolate. Drinking chocolate.

He smiled drowsily and looked at the sky.

'There's some fuzz,' Bos was shouting. 'Over there. The fuckers.'

'Yeah. Look at them.' Keith banged Francis on the shoulder and waded into the crowd behind Bos. They vanished immediately.

Another group burst from the Underground and Francis stared numbly at the swarming faces. Now he was alone, the crowd seemed even more enormous, more chaotic. He pressed to a lamp-post and hauled himself off the ground.

He saw a cresting wave of policemen on horses, and on the wall behind them a crisply painted sign: Park Lane, W1. A leisurely horse-drawn carriage clip-clopped through his head. Then he looked again and saw, filling the long road ahead, the central river of the demonstration. Here and there tributaries wriggled into Hyde Park, or into alleys and forecourts. They seemed agitated by their thinness, and wriggled frantically. Around them, tossed briefly out of the river and then sucked back again, a few isolated figures were splashed on to the pavement, or across a patch of brown grass, or up the trunk of a tree. Nothing they said was distinct. The main broad river drowned everything, flowing turgidly downhill.

But in fact it wasn't flowing downhill. It wasn't going anywhere at all. Just surging heavily to and fro, lapping and bulging, fed constantly by streams from neighbouring streets. Then a flurry swept towards him. The flick of faces turning together was like wind scoring the surface of the river, and although he didn't know what it meant, it thrilled him. It was definite and companionable. The bodies around him tensed, shouting more loudly. He wanted to shout too – shout what he had heard before and still didn't understand:

Ho, Ho, Ho Chi Minh.
Hot chocolate. Drinking chocolate.

He drifted easily away from the lamp-post. A pockmarked slab of curb flew under his feet. The fidgeting line of police horses rushed by like a cartoon. Were Keith and Bos there? Shoulders packed against him and the sky darkened. He was running now – so was everyone. The road shook with the pounding shuffle. He had started to make little barks. 'Hey,' he heard. 'Hey.' He crouched into a solid line with the shoulders either side of him. Who were they, these people? The man on his left had a broad bald head and was sweating heavily. The 'ch' of 'chocolate' shook a grey jet of saliva out of his mouth. He had a short black coat and he looked unconscious – awake but unconscious.

'Hi,' said a voice on his right. Francis turned to a square-jawed girl. Her black hair was pulled into a pony-tail, and a loose whisker flapped against her cheek. 'Hi,' she said again, her voice wobbling. 'I'm Miranda.'

Francis wondered which of his names to use. 'Frank,' he decided, nodding. A bead of sweat drooled down his cheek. The girl craned towards him; she was wearing a long brown coat which jumped around her as she ran. She wriggled a hand into the crook of his elbow.

'Hang on,' she shouted. 'Much easier like this when we get there.'

'Yes.' Francis felt witless.

'You from Oxford too?'

'Yes.'

'I think it's all Oxford, this lot.' She glanced at the sweating man. 'You met Reg?'

'Sort of.'

The crowd suddenly tightened down a side street, flooding round parked cars. Francis saw a radio aerial broken off and left to dangle, shuddering as people brushed against it like a twig snagged in a stream.

'How many of us?' Francis panted.

'Hundred. Hundred and fifty.'

'And altogether?'

'In the park? Thousands. Those bastards don't want us near the embassy like last time.' Miranda's face was glowing. She looks beautiful, Francis thought. How much older than me is she?

'Bastards,' he spat.

'How can we fight on two fronts?'

'We can't.' Francis didn't understand what he was saying, but when Miranda squeezed his arm through the thick sleeve of his coat he grinned at her. 'Bastards,' he said again.

The crowd concertinaed and Francis pitched violently into a dark-green overcoat. He smelt rain in its whiskery cloth. The weight of the crowd at his back was colossal.

Then Miranda was tugging at his arm. 'Here, Frank. Follow Reg.'

Reg had somehow slithered round the far side of Miranda, and Francis burrowed after him, letting go of Miranda and using his hands like a swimmer. His fingers brushed carelessly against sharp metal points, creamy cloth, hot flabby skin. Then he was by a black railing, looking down into a basement where there was a desk with a jug of yellow tulips on it, and a blank pad of paper. The crowd was looser here.

Reg stared without curiosity. 'It's the fucking fuzz,' he said in an arid voice. 'They've put the fucking barriers up round the fucking embassy again.' He gestured towards the head of the crowd, and as if it were a signal, the confused baying focused into a chant:

LBJ
Mur-*dur*-er
LBJ
Mur-*dur*-er

'Come on,' said Reg, leading the way along the railings. Francis bent double and burst into the light against a waist-high metal fence. It was absurd that such a flimsy thing should keep back such a crowd. These people pressing behind him – surely they could burst through whenever they chose? The line of police on the other side of the fence didn't stand a chance. In fact they looked like a row of actors, with their arms linked and their legs braced – as though they were about to sing, and hop from foot to foot. The square behind them, with its brown-leaved trees, and dark metal eagle poised on the roof of the embassy, was a ridiculous stage backdrop.

Francis leant his hands on the cool fence and examined the policeman in front of him. It was like inspecting the plumage of a bird he had seen every day of his life but never studied carefully before. He began with the man's boots – rubbery, with deep soles and no toe-caps. They looked vast. Then the trousers, slightly too short in the leg and slightly too long in the crotch. Then the tunic with its crested silver buttons.

The left-hand breast pocket contained a square bulge: a notebook. There was a narrow black stain at the bottom of the pocket. Ink. Francis had sometimes been taken to watch his father in uniform, inspecting soldiers. The brigadier would never have passed a stain like that.

He looked into the man's face. He was shockingly young under the high dome of his helmet – about twenty, with a fiercely folded lower lip and a little sore place just under his nose. He sniffed. He had a cold.

Francis turned to tell Miranda. 'Ssssssh.' Spray speckled his face and the chanting behind them faltered. From somewhere in the heart of the crowd, beginning with a few passionate voices then spreading quickly, came a pert song, briskly sung. Everyone knew it, and everyone joined in. It reached the front of the crowd and broke over Francis like a gust of rain. He knew the words too, and began to sing:

> One, two, three
> What are we fighting for?
> Don't ask me, I don't give a damn
> Next stop is Vietnam.
> Five, six, seven,
> Open up those pearly gates.
> There ain't no time to wonder why,
> Whoopee, we're all gonna die.

As soon as the song ended it began again, whisking along, louder each time, yet always amicable. Its lightness belonged with the comic policemen and the stage-prop embassy. But as it went on, the words became a babble of quick-trotting noises. Cold-hearted. The police stiffened their shoulders.

The song began again, the end of each line blending raggedly with the beginning of the next, hurrying to reach the final phrase. The crowd shifted in a single block.

> One, two, three

Reg was singing beside him, but in fact not singing. Shouting. Miranda's voice was lost to him.

Five, six, seven

Francis was hollow; the blunt bite of the fence was nothing.

Whoopee, we're all gonna die!

'Die' hammered between his shoulders – bitten off, only part of a word. He surfed forward on its high yelp, and the fence disappeared beneath him as if he had crashed into water and was kicking clear of wreckage. He clenched to strike his policeman, but didn't know whether he'd hit him or not. There were a few feeble snags and plucks at his legs, and that was all. It was like running through brambles. He was dizzy and closed his eyes. A hand was gripping his right arm; it must be Miranda. He whirled his other arm and when he struck cloth, hung on. His shirt burst open; cool air breathed on his chest; he hurtled forwards again.

When he opened his eyes he was outside the embassy – there was a cold shadow over everything, like the shadow outside the shops where he and Keith had met Bos. Why weren't they here now? Pimpled blue plastic covered the steps at his feet, and at the top was the darker blue line of more police. Each man held a gleaming wooden stick.

He struggled to focus. This wasn't his policeman, this shape in front of him. This was an older man, wearing a black metal hat like a motor-bike rider. He had a trim grey moustache and as Francis watched the mouth below, it suddenly opened into a small hard hole. He said bastard, Francis thought futilely. That policeman said bastard.

Miranda burst from his side, raising both fists as if she were impaling herself. There was a guttural sob, and a black glove tightened round one of her wrists. Then she lazily left the ground, hovered at shoulder height for a long moment and sank face-upward on to the steps, pop-eyed.

Francis understood what was going to happen next. He knew how the policemen either side of her would kneel down, how one would press on her shoulders, pinning her to the steps, and how the other one – the one with the moustache – would whip open her brown coat, draw off his glove, and flurry his hand under her skirt with a stiff, circling movement. It was all as he expected. Standing at the foot of the steps, arms hanging loosely, he might as well have been lounging at the back of an auditorium. He was a latecomer to this play he already knew. This act was drawing to an end and soon the next would begin.

Miranda screamed – a coarse scratching, as if something were scuttling down her throat – and suddenly he didn't know what to expect any more. Everything was new. A dense octopus struggle broke out around him and the two policemen were isolated, with Miranda still lying on the steps between them. How completely unlike Catherine she looks, Francis thought, as he loomed above her. Much older. Much thicker-set. One of his hands, stretching slowly forwards, came to rest on a shoulder. It belonged to the policeman, the one with the moustache. Next to him, Reg was tumbling the other policeman down the steps and out of sight like a bag of grain. Reg, too, seemed to be moving very slowly and easily. It was as if they were both underwater.

Francis watched his second hand float down on to the policeman and gently hoist him so that he was sitting on his haunches. Then Reg casually swept up his straightened right leg towards the policeman's face, and his shoe – a scuffed, pale-brown desert boot – wrinkled as it struck the cheekbone. The policeman's eye writhed in its socket like a marble juddering in a cup, and two dark-red fingers of blood poked out of his nose. Precisely as they appeared – when the blood was sticking a quarter of an inch out of the nostrils, when Reg's brown boot was still nuzzling the cheekbone, when his own hands were still resting on the policeman's shoulders – a white mackintosh flapped behind him, pointed a camera at their huddled tableau and flashed off a picture. For an instant Francis couldn't think what the brightness meant; when he understood, he had already seen the picture. It was on the front page of a newspaper, under a beetling headline. He let the policeman loll out of his hands and collapse down the steps. Miranda scrambled to her feet, brushing her coat. 'Bastards,' she said evenly. 'Bastards.' Reg melted. Francis buried himself in the crowd.

Halfway across the station car-park Francis heard Keith inside the bike-shelter, pulling his padlock-chain through the spokes with a tingling clatter. 'Oh, it's you,' Keith grunted, taken aback. He rallied at once. 'Where were you? We had the most amazing day, Bos and me. You should have been there. Really amazing.' He looped the chain round his handlebars and clicked the padlock shut.

Francis said nothing. Car doors slammed and engines started behind him. Yellow headlights flung his shadow along the mesh of the perimeter fence, the bike-shelter, then the fence again. For a moment Keith was caught like a spy crossing a frontier – only he was too well-groomed to be a spy, Francis thought. He had put his tie on, and his hair was combed. His overcoat collar was turned down.

The headlights melted and Keith came close, holding the bike between them. Francis noticed the seat had a tartan cover, like the rug on Catherine's bed. He glimpsed the brigadier tweaking tomorrow's newspaper out of the letter-box at home.

'Fucking a-mazing time,' Keith said. 'You know we went off to get those horses? Well, when we got there – though Jesus what a crush, it took ages – when we got there Bos started chucking the shit down in front of them and what do you think?'

'I give up,' Francis said immediately, shoving his hands into his overcoat pockets.

'Go on, guess.'

'I told you, I give up.'

Keith's face shone like a lantern. 'He was arrested! A policeman, one in ordinary clothes, just came out of the crowd and arrested him. "I must ask you to accompany me to the van, sir." Amazing. Just came up and said that. Arrested him. And what do you think for?'

128

'I've no idea.'

'Drugs!'

'Drugs?'

'Drugs!'

'I heard you.' Francis shrugged impatiently. It was cold, now the car-park was empty.

'I mean,' Keith laughed, 'they thought the lion's shit was shit, can you believe it? They thought it was cannabis he was throwing on the ground, pounds of it, and they busted him.'

'Didn't they think he was being a bit wasteful?'

'They can't think,' Keith said fiercely.

'Sounds to me as if they'd thought pretty carefully.'

'Isn't it amazing?'

'Sounds to me as if they thought he'd be trouble later, so they got him sooner, not later. Where is he now?'

Keith chortled. 'Oh well, it got worse. This guy who tried to arrest him, the one in plain clothes, he got Bos by the back of the neck and sort of steered him away, and Bos didn't fancy it, not surprisingly, and started to struggle. Struggle quite a lot in fact.' Keith chortled again. 'Fight, really, I suppose. He sort of swiped at him with the bag, so there was shit all over the place, and then the fuzz started going on about resisting arrest and Christ knows what.' He ran his hand wonderingly over the tartan cover of the bike seat and shook his head. 'In the end they just locked him in a van and drove him away, and that was that. No more Bos. Incredible, isn't it?'

Francis pursed his lips. 'So what did you do?'

'Oh, hung around, you know. Listened to some speeches. I tried to hear Tariq Ali, but I missed him, or maybe he wasn't there. I thought perhaps I might get to ... It's amazing how time goes.' He gave a shallow laugh. 'Next time I looked at my watch I had to come back.' Keith spun the top of the bell on his handlebars so it made a twangling ring. 'Why don't you get your bike, and you can tell me what you did on the way up?' He made as if to wheel forward, but Francis stood his ground.

'Well, as a matter of fact I ended up attacking the embassy.'

'You what?'

'I attacked the embassy in Grosvenor Square,' Francis repeated stubbornly. 'There were about three hundred of us, from Oxford, but I was with two of them really, and we went together.'

'From Oxford? What group were they from?' Keith leant across the bike.

'I didn't ask.'

'Trots, I expect,' Keith said, recovering himself. 'Bos said there'd be some Oxford Trots there.'

'They might have been. There wasn't much time for talking, actually, we were too busy.'

Keith narrowed his eyes. 'Attacking the embassy, you mean?'

'Well, it was more the police than the embassy. You can't just go up to a building and attack it, I mean, can you?'

'So you attacked the police?'

'Yes, but not all at once,' Francis ploughed on. 'Most of us attacked just one or two. I attacked the one in front of me – or really the girl I was with, Miranda, she attacked first and then Reg, he was another one I met, Reg and I attacked the policeman who'd attacked her. I held him, and Reg kicked him in the head. Someone took a picture but I'm pretty sure they didn't get my face, they were behind me. Then I went. I tried to find you but I didn't know where you were.'

Keith's smile wobbled in the darkness. 'No, well, I told you . . .'

Francis looked away, unclenching his hands in his pockets and flexing his fingers. He supposed a breeze must have sprung up, and that was why his eyes were blurred. But he couldn't hear a wind – there was nothing whispering through the mesh fence, or rattling the corrugated walls of the bike shelter.

'And after that I suppose you blew up the Houses of Parliament?' Keith said.

A bolt of anger struck Francis in the chest. 'OK, you want to know what I did after that? After that I went to the Natural History Museum, like we said we would. I didn't know what else to do. I spent the afternoon just mooning around. Listening to some audio-visual shit about monkeys. And do you know what I was thinking?'

'Francis.' Keith was holding out one hand like a child coming to the front of the class to be strapped.

'Fuck off, that wasn't a question. What I was thinking was how unfuckingbelievably pissed off with you I was for disappearing when the whole day had been your idea in the first place. I didn't want to go. I mean: I didn't mind going, but I didn't want it to be like that. It was out of control. I don't care about Vietnam or anything – well, I do care, but not like that. And you know what? I don't think you care either. I think the whole thing's just one enormous wank. Just a huge wank.'

Francis ran out of breath. He stared at the rippled back wall of the bike-shelter and imagined his words piled up against it, jumbled and squeaking like bats in a cave. He had contradicted himself and he couldn't understand why. His legs were trembling, his knees tapping the cloth of his trousers. Keith must have seen; it must be why he was smiling.

'Understand?' Francis blurted finally.

'I'm not sure,' said Keith slowly, his head on one side. His breath was rich. Wine? 'What did you do after that?'

Francis searched Keith's face but there was no warmth in it, and he knew he had lost. It was him, not Keith, who felt a fool. 'I went to the station,' he said weakly. His shoulders slumped; they ached.

Keith straddled his bike, bent forward and twiddled something Francis couldn't see. The small, hard beam of a lamp leapt across the car-park. Then he leant back like a jockey taking a fence and a red glow appeared beside the back wheel. He cocked a pedal, braced his arms on the handlebars and turned to Francis. Their faces were only inches apart.

He's going to kiss me, Francis thought. He's forgiven me for what I've said and now we're going to start again. We're going to be like we were before. Before Catherine died.

'By the way,' Keith drawled, 'your mother sends you her love.' There was a spurt of gravel and the red back-light shot away into the darkness, jiggling crazily over the ruts at the gate on to the main road.

Next morning Francis tore the page out of the paper before breakfast. He showed it to Alex and Jamie, but they didn't recognize him in the photograph. He wasn't surprised; he was just a jellyfish hand on the policeman's shoulder. The policeman himself was flawless: his juddering eye, his stiff moustache, his fingers spread as he tried to protect his face.

'Poor sod,' said Jamie, gangling over the page. 'Think what his kids must feel like, seeing that.'

'It doesn't say he's got any kids.'

'No, but I bet he has. Don't you think?' Jamie winced away.

Francis said nothing about the picture to Keith, and did his best to avoid him. It was difficult; they kept passing each other in corridors, or glimpsing each other across rooms. But their anger held, and gradually began to look like indifference. Keith belonged in the past, Francis insisted; he was history.

The sky hardened into November, with slate clouds roofing the valley. At the end of the month, Adele came down. She promised to arrive at twelve thirty, but there was fog and she didn't appear until two. If Keith had heard she was coming, there was no sign of him as Francis climbed into the Mini.

They probed along the valley to Abingdon, their headlights washing the drizzly hedges. Adele announced that she would have to leave soon, the weather was so bad. Francis said he understood. In the Crown and Thistle they drank coffee in a garish, empty room overlooking the river – too late for lunch, too early for tea. The hotel was popular with parents visiting their children, and occasionally a boy hovered in the doorway. 'Oh, hallo, Mayne, didn't know you were here. Sorry.'

Adele had thought it best to dress cheerfully, and was wearing an orange trouser-suit, with a quilted Indian waistcoat thrown on over the jacket, because of the cold. The waistcoat was tight, and her arms and legs stuck out like a doll's.

'Are you cold, darling? I'm freezing.' She massaged her arms.

'No, I'm fine, thanks.' Francis stared through cramped mullions at the river. The soaked ghosts of rowing boats huddled against the far bank; their wetness was painful to look at. Shavings of fog gusted across the water, clung together for a moment or two, then listlessly swirled apart. The damp crept into his bones.

'Are you sure you're not cold, darling?'

'Sure.'

Adele stopped rubbing herself and leant forward confidentially. 'Perhaps you're sickening for something?'

Francis continued to look down at the black river. 'I don't think so.'

They tunnelled back as darkness fell, Francis peering blindly ahead, saying nothing. He had wasted Adele's time. He had made her take a dangerous journey. They hadn't talked about Catherine. They hadn't talked about Keith.

'Are you *sure* you're all right, Effie?' Adele asked as they turned into the drive. 'You haven't got a tummy-ache or anything?' She sounded exasperated.

'No, honestly, I'm fine, thanks.' Francis straightened. 'Don't bother to come all the way up, will you. Just drop me here; I'm perfectly happy to walk.' The Mini slowed. 'It'll make you later than ever.'

'It's only a minute or two.'

'Please,' Francis insisted. 'I'd like to walk. You might get stuck, you know, talking to people.'

'What do you mean, talking to people?' Adele asked narrowly. There was saliva in the corner of her mouth.

'Oh, I don't know,' Francis blinked. 'Keith.'

'I wouldn't mind seeing him again; I rather liked him. He seemed very grown up.' Her voice was loud and enthusiastic in the bubble of the car. 'He's still your friend is he? You haven't talked about him.'

'No, well, we've both been very busy, you know.'

'You mean his university thing? Give him good luck from me, will you?' The Mini groaned as Adele braked and took it out of gear. 'Perhaps he might come and see us in the holidays. Joe wouldn't mind.'

The windscreen-wipers whirred and clunked. 'I suppose we'd better get the holidays sorted out, hadn't we?' Francis said heavily. 'Where I'm going to be.'

'No need to worry about that,' Adele said. 'Though actually, darling, it might be best if you came to me first, because Joe says he might take me away somewhere, you know, for Christmas and the New Year. Somewhere warm – that would be rather nice, wouldn't it?'

Francis gazed up the drive. The chestnut avenue reared out of the fog like a child's drawing of ghosts. 'We'll sort it out, I'm sure,' he muttered. 'Goodbye.' He made no effort to get out.

'Goodbye, darling.' Adele was twisting her wedding ring round her finger. 'The time's gone so fast.' She sniffed. 'I'm sorry.'

'Why sorry?'

'It's just that we never seem to talk about anything any more. We never seem to say anything.' She was tearful, but Francis couldn't think how to answer her. 'About what you're doing, and your friends. And work. And the magazine.' She pulled herself together. 'I mean, take the magazine. You haven't told me a thing about it.'

'It isn't important,' said Francis. The fog seemed to be thinning. The chestnut trees no longer looked frightening but derelict, like extinguished chandeliers.

'It is, darling,' Adele urged. 'It's terribly important.'

'It isn't.'

'Now you're being silly,' she said sharply. 'It must matter to you, otherwise you wouldn't do it. I don't just mean the magazine, I mean everything. Work. Everything you do. It's your life.'

Francis shook his head. 'No it isn't. What I do isn't my life.'

'What on earth do you mean? Of course what you do is your life.'

'No it isn't,' Francis said carefully, as if he was speaking from memory. 'What I've done so far hasn't been my life. What I do isn't what I think about.'

Adele turned off the wipers and drizzle covered the windscreen in a luminous fur.

'None of us talks about what we do,' Francis went on. 'In school, I mean. School and teachers and classrooms and lessons and games and prep. It's a sort of thing with us.'

Adele sucked in her bottom lip with an irritable slurp. 'Well, it's a very funny sort of thing. Very funny. And you're very lucky, that's all I can say. Very lucky to be so clever, you and your friends, that you don't have to talk about work.' She clicked on the wipers and revved the engine impatiently. 'It makes it so hard to get near you, darling. You ought to talk about things, you really ought.'

'I told you. We do talk – just not about what we do, you know.'

'I don't really know, I must admit.' She paused, baffled, then suddenly twinkled at him. 'You mean girls, don't you?'

'In a way.' Francis swallowed and the chestnuts pranced at him, holding up their gleaming branches like hysterics. The grey drive, dwindling where the headlights faded, was entrancingly bare.

'I didn't mean it to be like this,' Francis said rapidly. 'I think I'd better go. I've made you late enough as it is.' He clambered out, slammed the door and bent to the window. Crouching below him, Adele looked a long way away, or a long time ago, in black and white, smiling a big uncomplicated smile. She thinks she's won, he realized. She thinks I'm guilty, and she's triumphant.

'Goodbye,' she mouthed from deep in the car. Francis said, 'Thank you' before he could stop himself.

By the time she turned into the road he had started to run. 'The bitch,' he said aloud. 'The selfish, lying bitch.' The words kept time with the smacks of his shoes on the tarmac, then with the thump of frozen grass as he shied off the drive under the chestnuts. 'The selfish lying bitch.' He wasn't clear what he meant.

He cannoned through the door into Jamie's study corridor and a voice shouted, 'Oh, for fuck's sake.' Another voice, cutting across it, snarled, 'Shut that fucking door or I'll kill you, whoever you are.' Francis stopped, panting. Under a row of dim lights, two boys were transfixed holding coffee cups, staring at him as he knocked on Jamie's door. There was no answer and he went in. The air was dusty; it hadn't been disturbed for hours. Pushkin glowed at him like a knowing monkey. He clicked his tongue and stepped back into the corridor. The two boys were still there, steam curling from their fists.

'No sign.' Francis half-laughed, as if he didn't care.

One of the boys, ignoring Francis completely, turned to the other and said, 'Do you think he doesn't know?'

Francis pushed past them and burst out into the fog again, towards his own study.

Alex was sitting with his back to the door, his jacket straining across his monumental shoulders. He was listening to music through a pair of plump black headphones. Francis ruffled his hair.

'Christ!' Alex snatched off the headphones, blushing. 'You nearly made me jump out of my fucking skin.'

Francis dropped into the chair under the window, resting his hands on its bare wooden arms. 'I didn't know how else to make you hear.'

'No, well . . .' Alex sulked, and the tinny whisper expired. 'It'd nearly finished anyway.'

'What is it?'

'Hendrix,' he said, his craggy face beaming. '"All Along

the Watchtower". Amazing. I went in to Oxford this afternoon and got it. Pissing awful day.' Alex was clipped, his knees pressed nervously together.

'What's up?'

'You haven't heard, then?' Alex fingered the black wire dangling from the headphones.

'What is it, for Christ's sake?' Francis felt his insides soften. Adele flounced through his head.

'It's that shit Middleton,' Alex said tautly, staring at the desk-top. 'He caught Shagger O'Brien laying a bomb, or whatever you do to bombs. Planting one. He took him to the head, and he's been expelled, Shagger has.'

Francis was smiling, his mouth curling like paper in a fire.

'And that isn't the end of it,' Alex went on hurriedly. 'Not by a long chalk. Because before he went . . '

'He's actually gone, has he?'

'I'll tell you. Before he went, he told the head about Gower being his partner, and they went to look for Gower. They found him in bed with Jamie, and they've both been expelled too, Gower and Jamie have.'

'Jamie's been expelled?'

'Yes.'

'That's why I couldn't find him.'

'What?' Alex looked at Francis, but their eyes didn't meet.

'I've just been to his study looking for him.' Francis lifted one hand off the wooden arm of his chair and gazed at the sweaty imprint of his palm. 'Actually expelled?' he said, forcing himself to frown. 'But what for? He didn't have anything to do with the bombs.'

'I don't know. Being queer.' Alex shrugged and his chair creaked pitifully. 'Corrupting younger boys.'

'Gower wasn't younger,' Francis said fiercely.

Alex laughed, straightening his legs. 'I don't suppose anybody really minds much.'

Francis was confused. He wanted to run out and stand in the open, in the middle of the playing fields in the darkness, and think what it meant. It wasn't like death. It was ridiculous, wasn't it? Even a bit exciting. But it was something other than that, too. Not to have Jamie there any more. Not to hear his voice. His chest heaved.

'You OK?' Alex said cautiously. 'I mean, I know you two . . .'

'It'll kill his parents,' Francis interrupted softly.

'It'd kill anybody's.'

'No, but especially his.'

'I don't think . . .'

'His Dad's a senior bean in the National Trust. You know, they live in some bloody old pile in Wiltshire. View of the church and everything. They just won't believe it. His mother's made entirely of tweed. It'll kill them.'

'Shit,' Alex sighed. 'I can just see it.'

'He's their only child,' Francis said under his breath, then roused himself. 'Just tell me everything about it, will you?'

'I don't know it all.' Alex rubbed his cheeks as if testing whether he needed a shave. 'I'd been in Oxford, like I said, so I didn't actually see any of it. But I think what happened was that Shagger was trying to blow a hole in the infirmary – you know how everyone had been on to him about Sister Limm's hot spoon after you wrote that song, telling him he'd had it and everything? Well, he was round there by the infirmary, where the laurels are, with the bomb in his hand . . .'

'Oh?' Francis smiled again and Alex, relieved, grinned broadly. 'Yes, apparently it was a real bomb – a black ball with BOMB written on it in white, and a wick coming out of the top.'

'I saw a wick once,' Francis said in a far-away voice. 'Shagger showed me.'

'Did he? Great! You never told me.'

'In the music school. Anyway, go on.'

'Well, there he was, like an assassin, when along comes the winnet Middleton. Apparently he'd been on to Shagger for ages, or so he says now. He just wanted proof. He's chuffed as hell of course, the bollock. He took him straight along to the head, and he was expelled there and then.' Alex paused, his smile melting. 'But first he was beaten.'

'Fuck.' Blood rushed into Francis' face. 'How many?'

'Six, I think. They all were. Beaten.'

Francis clamped his hands over the arms of his chair, his balls prickling. Would they have had to take their trousers down, he wanted to know? He saw Jamie's loose body stooping, his white arse blooming into the cold light of the head's window overlooking the lake.

'It's disgusting,' Alex spat. 'Disgusting.'

Francis said nothing and eventually Alex's chair creaked again. 'Shall I go on?' he asked.

'Sure,' Francis whispered. 'Go on.'

'Well, Middleton went to look for Gower because Shagger must have told by then, and they found him with Jamie, like I said.'

'Actually in bed?' Francis asked, matter-of-fact.

'Yes, in Jamie's bed, in his dorm.'

'Just like that, in the middle of the afternoon? Jamie must be mad.'

'They were asleep,' Alex said, with a little bubble of laughter. 'Middleton said it was rather hard to wake them up. He had to shout at them. He said they must have been worn out.'

'I bet he did, the shit,' Francis said vehemently. 'But have they already gone? I mean, can I say goodbye or something?'

'I don't know about Jamie; I only know about Shagger.' Alex twitched.

Francis frowned. 'What about him, then?'

'He didn't say goodbye. Just sat in his study waiting for his Dad.'

'God; his Dad,' said Francis distractedly. 'I don't think I'd even thought he had a Dad.'

'That's the thing,' said Alex, suddenly swelling. 'He arrived in a hearse. He's an undertaker.'

'An undertaker? Jesus.' Francis blinked. 'Anything in it – in the hearse? Any coffins?'

Alex was grinning uncontrollably. 'No, in fact Shagger

slung his things in the back where coffins go, and they vamoosed. Shagger's Dad didn't even turn off the engine.'

'There must be more to it than that. How fast, for instance?'

'Pretty fast, since you ask.' Alex glanced at Francis, as if seeking permission to go on. 'Like the clappers, actually,' he ventured.

'More.'

'I reckon old Shagger's Dad must have been touching fifty by the time they were halfway down the drive.'

'Fifty? In the fog?'

'Well, forty-five, then. Fast, anyway. Shagger's stuff was fairly shooting around in the back.'

'They're very slippery, the backs of hearses.'

'I dare say.' Alex wiped his forehead. 'Shagger's Dad looked furious. He just signalled for Shagger to get in and they set off.'

'Anyone see?' Francis asked squeakily.

'Oh yes.' Alex wagged a finger at Francis. 'I ought to have told you about that. As the hearse went – it sort of rocketed off, really, you could see Shagger tossed back in his seat – there was quite a lot of applause from the studies.'

'People in their windows?'

'Yes, but you know, sort of hanging out of them. Seeing Shagger off.'

'His Dad must have liked that.'

'Don't suppose he heard it.' Alex gave a huge shrug, and the silver paper crackled on the walls. 'He was making such a row with his engine. He was gunning it like mad; there were clouds of exhaust.'

'What sort of applause?'

'Oh, you know. Clapping, mainly. Quite a lot of cheering. Lister or someone gave a most terrific fart on his bassoon.'

'Shagger's Dad must have heard that.'

'If he did, he'd have thought it was an angel blowing off.'

Francis wiped a tear from his eye, his laughter leaving him. 'You'd have thought he might have come in his own car, wouldn't you.'

'It is his own car, you arsehole,' Alex said seriously. 'He must have been out on a job and come straight from work.'

Francis laughed again, but the air had been pressed out of him. He put his hands on his knees. 'He must live locally.'

'He must. It's bad not to know, isn't it?'

'Very bad. I did ask him about his people once, but he wouldn't tell me. Isn't his mother dead?'

'Christ knows. We must write to him or something. Poor old Shagger.'

'Poor Shagger.'

There was a pause, then Alex said quietly, 'Oh, and one other thing. As he went, Shagger shouted something. It sounded like, "I'll get you, you bastards." Something like that, anyway. "I'll get you," was obviously what he meant.'

Francis folded his hands on his lap. 'They're mad buggers, these Irish.'

'Is he Irish? He doesn't sound it.'

'Must be, mustn't he, with a name like that?' Francis smiled to himself. 'I rather like the idea of this being the start of Shagger's life of crime. Can't you just see him, blowing things up here and there?'

'Here and where, though?'

'Oh, I don't know. Everywhere. He'll find a reason.'

They stared at the empty space between them. Alex was slouched, his hands flopped in his lap. Francis began to read a face in the scribbles of coffee on the carpet.

'It's kind of hard to know what to feel, isn't it?' Alex said at last.

'I don't think so,' said Francis decisively. 'I think it's terrible. Just terrible.'

'Yes, well, it is, of course. Of course it's terrible. But I mean, at least they're out of this dump.'

'But what will they do? What about the rest of their lives?'

Alex crossed his heavy thighs like a secretary about to take a letter. 'They'll be all right. They always are, these people. They'll go to crammers or something and then carry on as normal. All it means is they get to smoke cigarettes and screw girls sooner than we do.'

'You can keep the girls,' Francis snarled. 'What do you think Jamie would do with girls, for Christ's sake?'

Alex straightened. 'Well, he can go to a crammer and screw boys, then, can't he,' he said petulantly. 'I don't think he's exactly vanished from your life for ever, if that's what you're worrying about. I expect the National Trust will come to the rescue. His Dad'll get him a job as an architect or something – you'll see. They're all poofs who do that.'

Francis glowered at Alex. 'Oh yes, I expect so,' he said bitterly. 'I expect you're absolutely right.' With no warning Catherine's voice broke in on him. 'You don't know whether to laugh or cry,' she was saying. Where had that been? It had been open air, with grass stewing in the sun. Could it be the cricket match? 'I mean,' he said, 'it's not as if you don't know whether to laugh or cry.'

Alex looked up at him steadily. 'What's that got to do with anything? Anyway, don't get Bolshie with me about it. It's not my fault.'

'I know that.' Francis was still blazing. 'I'm just saying, that's all.'

'Well, they were making bombs, I mean it's . . .'

'Jesus, Alex, whose side are you on? I know. Bombs. But, I mean, beaten. Beaten for being queer. These people are our friends. I'm telling you. It's bloody barbaric.'

'I know that, now calm down.'

'No I bloody well won't calm down.' Francis threw himself towards the door without knowing where he was going.

Alex's curly black hair and puzzled face drifted by far below him. 'You better *had* calm down,' he was saying. 'Because your friend wants to see you. If he still is your friend, that is.'

Francis paused. 'What do you mean?'

'I mean there's another bit I still haven't told you, and if you'll just shut up for a moment and stop ranting, then I will.' Alex turned his back and switched on the record-player.

'Your friend Jamie told the head that your friend Keith Ogilvie was mixed up with the bomb factory.' He picked up the white plastic arm. 'I can't think why, can you? Well perhaps you can. Anyway, according to Middleton, the head had Keith in, but amazingly he ended up convinced that Jamie had been talking bollocks. Not surprisingly, though, Keith was pretty pissed off, and wondered whether you knew anything about it. So he's looking for you.' Alex put the earphones over his head and lowered the needle on to the record. There was the miniature noise of someone jumping on gravel. 'He's waiting for you now,' Alex said, knowing he wouldn't be able to hear an answer.

Keith was sprawled on the bed of red cushions in the alcove – awkward yet utterly relaxed, like the body of a suicide. Francis thrust the door shut and Keith inflated, scrabbling towards him what looked like scrumpled paper and chocolate.

'What the fucking hell do you think you're doing, bursting in without knocking?' His voice was choked. 'And what the fucking hell are you staring at?'

'I did knock,' said Francis. 'And I was staring at your drugs. At least, I suppose drugs is what they are. This place stinks like a cat tray.'

'"Your drugs",' Keith minced. 'How quaint. This is Moroccan Gold, not that you'll know what that is.'

'I do, as a matter of fact.' Francis sat at the desk. It was immaculate – everything in its place, everything as it had always been. The neat piles of notepaper; the camera; the ink bottle; the green glass jar with its yellow pencils.

'Oh yeah, how?' said Keith, sinking back into the cushions.

'Oh yeah; Jamie,' said Francis. He was pleased with the lie; it told him he was in charge.

'I see we're not wasting time. I suppose Roberts told you what happened.'

'In a general sort of way.' Francis looked round unhurriedly; the silver pixies writhed on their poster. 'It's bloody hot in here. Do you mind if I open a window?' He fiddled the latch before Keith could answer, and looked out. The fog had lifted and on the playing fields below the airy, luminous H of a rugger post pulsed in the darkness.

Keith flung up his right arm to cradle his head; his white shirt was open to the middle of his chest and his shoes were off. A sour whiff of leather mingled with the other scent. 'The silly bugger,' he murmured, staring at the ceiling. 'The poor silly bugger.'

'Poor, not silly,' said Francis tartly.

'Pretty sodding silly saying I was making bombs.'

'I'd have thought you'd be pleased. Doesn't it make you sound like a revolutionary?'

'I'm not a revolutionary,' Keith barked.

'Anyway. You got off.'

'There wasn't anything for me to get off. Remember?'

'No, well, you know what I mean.' Francis was momentarily flustered.

'Say what you mean, Frank. Always say what you mean.' Keith crouched forward; his eyes were red-rimmed and cloudy, the large pupils edged with a thin margin of brown.

Francis said, 'I expect Jamie meant it as a joke,' and immediately knew he had made a mistake. Keith would never understand a joke might be serious. If he'd known that Jamie had acted simply out of dislike he might have respected him. He knew about jealousy. What he didn't understand was the different ways in which things could be ridiculous.

'Well, as a serious joke, I mean,' he added hurriedly, but it was too late. Keith had flung himself back on the cushions and closed his eyes.

Francis felt as if the whole tower was on the move, slicing through the evening like the periscope of a submarine cutting through water. He had come up here to argue, but he hadn't even started. When the chance arose he had retreated. A hand of wind slid round the window and caressed his face. It was the same as ever. He knew he was right, but Keith made him a fool.

He cleared his throat. 'Look, I . . .' he began; but Keith had fallen asleep, his wide mouth pouting. Francis lingered over his shirt, then moved to the dark gash of his chest, and down to his crotch. The slack ridge of his cock was negligible.

'Christ, sorry, Frank.' Keith spluttered and sat up. 'Must have nodded off there. Was I out for long?'

Francis shrugged.

'Shall I roll another one? Just a little one, maybe, because I'm already a bit . . .' He dismantled a cigarette, his hand stumbling among the tobacco, scraping it into a trough. When his fingers rubbed together, like a fly cleaning its legs, Francis saw Mrs Banyard by the Aga at home, crumbling a stock cube into a metal roasting dish. He heard an empty dish rattling on to the kitchen floor. Catherine had just died.

'I suppose Bos gave it to you, did he?' Francis asked.

'Sold it. Sold it to me. Yeah.' Keith ran his dark tongue along the side of the joint he had made, tucked it tight and offered it to Francis. 'Blow that weed,' he said dully.

'No thanks.'

'What?' Keith looked hot; his glossy hair had slithered into his eyes.

'I just don't feel like it.'

'Thought you said you did.' Keith lit a match and stared at it as if he had forgotten what it was for. 'All the more for me. Though it is only a little one. Just a tiny little one,' he said in a silly singsong, then lit up and dropped the blazing match into a coffee cup at his feet. It raged and went out as he settled back on the cushions.

'In-cred-ible,' he sighed at last, releasing the smoke in fussy puffs.

Francis shook his head. 'Keith. Are you listening?'

'Mmmm.' Keith gulped another lungful of smoke, flat on his back.

'I'm sure Jamie didn't mean to get you into trouble. I'm sure he knew you'd get off.'

Keith lay still, his cheeks sucked in. Then he breathed out a long whoosh. 'Listen, Frank. I've sorted that dreary little tart, don't you worry. I've sorted him. I'll admit I was annoyed to start with, but you're quite right, he couldn't hurt a gnat. I wanted to see you about it, when it first happened, but now I'd rather not talk about it.' He switched a smile on and off. 'OK?'

'What do you mean, you've sorted him?' Francis asked. A second, colder hand of wind slipped round the window.

'You'll see.' Smoke clawed out of Keith's mouth. 'Though there is one thing that baffles me, which is why you hung around with him as much as you did. With Jamieson. Wasn't he just an arsehole, and doing this proves it? A tarty little arsehole? I mean, we all went up there, didn't we? When I went up there I expected to find graffiti on the walls.' Keith flicked the roach of his joint into his coffee cup and shut his eyes. 'Graffiti on the walls,' he repeated slowly. 'I mean, I know he was your friend, and I'd like to understand, I really would.' He gave a shuddering gasp, like someone trying to stop weeping, then whispered with a final effort. 'But I've sorted him, you'll see. In fact, you could see now, if you wanted.' He sipped enough air to chortle, then his mouth sagged open and he was asleep.

Francis stood up, gripping Keith by the lapels and hoisting him off the cushions, then dropping him heavily back. There was no sign of consciousness. A white string of saliva, stretched between Keith's lips, vibrated as his breath wheezed to and fro. 'Lost to the world,' Francis said aloud, and glared round the room as if someone else had spoken. There was silence – no voices filtering up from the dormitories below, the velvet air stagnant over the playing fields, the posters clinging tightly to the walls. A few minutes ago Keith had looked like a suicide. Then hollow-cheeked, like someone drowning. Now, with his head and torso on the cushions and floppy doll's legs twisting on to the floor, he seemed to have fallen from an enormous height.

There were so many ways of being dead, and looking something like this. You could be Bobby, gunned down in front of a TV camera. Or you could be smashed into cobbles, leaking a raspberry of blood. Or you could be Catherine, fading like a chalk figure which the grass steadily covers on a hillside. Or you could be naked, sprinting down a long bare road with your hair scorched and brown blobs all over your body. Or you could be a perfectly blank gaze from a cross, then a relaxed bundle on the ground – something that must be covered and taken away in secret.

Keith swallowed, his lips slumping together, then parting with a hollow pop. Francis smiled. It would be in his desk, of course, whatever he had meant; he must have wanted him to find it. Francis dragged aside the chair and went through the drawers methodically. In the bottom right were two brown envelopes, one twice the size of the other. He took out the smaller one and fidgeted his finger under the flap.

The photographs slithered on to the desk-top like the gleaming guts of a fish. He pawed at them, splaying them out, and glimpsed slivers of his cock, his tense, peering face. The negatives were there too – a hard wad with an elastic band round them. He held one up to the desk-lamp and saw the white pompom of his black pubic hair. He smiled again – a slow, hearty smile – and slid the photographs back. Then he pulled the second, larger envelope out from Keith's desk. Inside it, as well as photographs and a little wad of negatives, was a single sheet of paper with three lines typed on it.

Dear Mr and Mrs Jamieson,
Now that your son has left I feel you should have some mementoes of his time away from

He folded the sheet of paper and tucked it into an inside pocket with Jamie's envelope. He put his own envelope into another pocket. He knew exactly what to do. Keith had made everything so simple. Keith, who understood everything that no one else understood. Clever Keith. Francis tiptoed to the door, leaning against it to make sure it was shut. With each step the photographs moved like plates of armour. Or like the scales of a fish. He was a fish walking – bizarre, magical, unlike himself. He picked the camera off the desk and stooped above Keith, squinting through the viewfinder. The fallen body was grey and minute, still grossly asleep, the mouth still open, the white strand of saliva still soundlessly vibrating.

On the last evening there was a carol service and it snowed. From the dark crevice of his pew Francis watched large flakes leafing the chapel windows, and imagined his voice travelling deserted pathways outside, fading through the softening branches of trees. Once he glanced at the reredos. It glowed meekly, like a fire which warmed but could not burn. Only the large central panel with its forlorn skeleton was distinct, but he didn't want to dwell on it. He let the whole elaborate structure blaze out of focus.

It snowed on and off during the night, and when he woke the bell clanking for breakfast sounded brittle. Only a few hours left now, he thought; it felt like the beginning of something, not the end.

By mid-morning, with his goodbyes done, he was in the study waiting for Rex to make his final round. He nodded at a cardboard box of records. 'Must weigh a ton.'

'Complete ton.' Alex was sitting tensely at his desk. 'You OK?'

'Me OK? Course I'm OK. Why shouldn't I be?'

'I don't know. You look a bit pukey.'

'Pukey? Thanks. I'm a bit cold, that's all.' Francis shrugged in his clean suit. He could hear Rex next door; there was the pausing murmur of a conversation, a click, shoes sucking along the corridor, then a light knock.

'Come in,' he and Alex said together, jerking to their feet.

'Aaah.' Rex sounded as if he hadn't expected to find them in. He was pink-faced in a thick tweed suit, his unruly brown hair brushed into a precarious crest. Under one arm was a copy of the magazine.

'Oh, hallo, sir,' Francis said, also pretending surprise.

'All tidy?' Rex swung his head, but with the three of them standing up it was impossible to see much. He trailed a finger along Alex's desk-top, then put his hand in his trouser pocket without looking at it. 'Christmas at home is it, Alexander?'

'Well, no, sir, not exactly.' Tucking himself into a corner, Alex rasped the heel of one shoe against a skirting board; there was a prickle of flaking paint and he blushed a painful crimson. 'We always go skiing in France for Christmas, sir. My sister's married to a Frenchman you see, and . . .'

'I believe you told me. Will this be before or after your . . .' Rex smiled, 'your audition?'

'Oh, before, sir,' Alex said enthusiastically. 'That's not until the new year. It seems the people at Parlophone . . .'

'Parlophone?' Rex queried.

'That's the company, sir. The people there have rather a long break at Christmas, so we're not seeing them till just before we come back.'

'I suppose you mean *if* you come back, don't you?' Rex asked, still smiling faintly. 'I suppose if you sign up . . .'

'Oh no, sir,' Alex was completely serious. 'We've all decided to finish here as normal, and then . . .'

'Ah, well, that's a relief, isn't it?' Rex turned to Francis. 'He'll still favour us with his presence.' His voice softened. 'And what about you? You'll be with your father, I expect.'

'That's right, sir. Though it's my mother collecting.' He glanced at the window as if he expected to see it framing Adele's beautiful, feline face.

'Very nice too,' Rex said. 'We can't all go around breaking our legs on mountains, can we?'

'Oh, I wouldn't say we all break our legs, sir,' Alex butted in cheerily, but Rex appeared not to hear him, and blinked at the carpet. Raw light swilled through the room, coating them with a feeble whitewash. They're thinking about Catherine, Francis realized.

Abruptly, Rex snatched the magazine from under his arm and began riffling the pages. 'I can't go without saying another word about this,' he said in a forced, dull voice. 'I expect you've looked at it by now, Alexander, have you? It really is well done. Really very well done.' Francis stepped backwards until the edge of his desk pressed into his legs. Outside car engines were slowing down and doors banged. 'Keith Ogilvie's essay,' Rex murmured. 'Really remarkable . . . remarkable . . . poems . . . Hardcastle's drawings for the sports . . .' He twisted the open magazine towards Francis as if he might not have seen it before. '*Very* good.'

'Good, sir.' Francis hadn't meant to whisper; he should have cleared his throat.

'Very witty,' Rex went on, turning a few more pages. 'And this competition section here at the end. Really very good. Very entertaining. A real innovation. I shall enjoy Rivers' crossword.' Rex chuckled, and Francis glimpsed Rivers walking in the sun last summer, yanking his head backwards and forwards by the forelock. 'And the Mystery Photograph.' Rex chuckled again, bringing the page close to his pink face then holding it at arms' length. 'Really, I've no idea. None at all.' He glanced up, pursing his lips. 'A bomb-crater? A dry pond?' He passed the magazine to Alex like a priest handing the Bible to an acolyte. 'Do you have any thoughts? Or perhaps you've been let in on the secret?'

Francis fingered the edge of his desk. It was greasy; his fingers must be sweating.

'Oh no, sir, certainly not.' Alex canted heavily forward. 'Water going down a plughole, sir?' he said in his large voice. 'There is a sort of twist, isn't there? Or perhaps it's one of those things blown up hundreds of times?'

'Things blown up?' Rex echoed nervously.

'Yes, sir, you know. A hair or something.'

'I see,' Rex took back the magazine, poking it under his arm again, then clasping his hands behind his back. He looked contorted. 'You've given us a great deal to think about, Francis,' he declared. 'A great deal. We shall have to scrutinize and ponder, shan't we, Alexander?'

'Yes, sir.'

'Scrutinize and ponder.' Rex rocked on his heels and the thick soles of his shoes sighed energetically. Francis felt a sudden flash of sadness. After they'd all gone, what would Rex do? Didn't he have a sister somewhere, and a cottage in Wales? He imagined a heathery hillside, and two bowed figures toiling through grey rain. 'I hope you have a good holidays, sir, and a happy Christmas.'

'That's right, sir,' Alex was enthusing. 'Happy Christmas, sir.'

'Thank you,' said Rex. 'And you.' He swirled round and was gone.

'Fucking hell.' Alex slumped at his desk, his arms dangling between his legs.

'Sssssh.'

'He can't hear us.' Alex was scornful, but lowered his voice. 'What the hell was he going on about the magazine like that for? I mean, he's said all that stuff to you about a million times. I thought he'd never bloody stop.'

Francis sat on his desk and wiped one hand over his face as though cleaning off a cobweb. 'He was just embarrassed or something.'

'Embarrassed?'

'Yeah, you know.' Francis couldn't be bothered to explain.

Alex twisted his head sideways. 'Hang on a minute . . .' He peered through the window. 'Yes it is. My old man's here.' He was on his feet, packing the space between his desk and the door.

Francis swivelled round and saw Alex in twenty years' time: a huge dark-green overcoat like a slab of wet rock; a thick neck and purplish face, curly hair tamed and streaked with grey.

'He looks well, anyway,' Francis said tritely.

Alex laughed. 'It's what comes of standing outside all day, losing your temper with the weather. You know farmers . . .'

Francis couldn't think of anything to say.

'Well, I'd better go, I suppose,' Alex went on uncertainly.

'Will you be here if I just pop out? I know he'd love to see you.'

Francis remembered something he'd read about travellers leaving on ocean liners. They threw paper streamers to friends on the dockside, and as the ship pulled away, the streamers tautened, strained and eventually snapped. When this happened the travellers knew they had left. The air hardened between himself and Alex. 'It's very nice of you, but I've got one or two things . . . you know.'

'Keith, you mean, to see,' Alex said clumsily.

'I thought I'd go up and say goodbye, yes.'

'You won't know what to do, will you, not being able to go up there all the time any more.' Alex gave a diffident laugh. 'I mean, going up there has sort of come after everything, hasn't it?'

Francis smiled and said nothing.

'Well, then.' Alex laughed again. 'Goodbye, I suppose.'

'I'll get out of your way.' Francis darted forward and Alex dodged, so it was not his cheek Francis kissed but the hard rim of his ear. Alex blushed fiercely as they stood apart.

'We might even talk,' Francis said without concentrating. How touching Alex looked! His rumpled hair. His mouth hanging slightly apart in that pitted, embarrassed face.

'Yeah,' said Alex, looking away.

Francis snatched a copy of the magazine from his desk and lunged into the corridor. 'Happy Christmas!' he shouted over his shoulder. The air between them snapped and he was free, weaving through the thickening swarm of boys towards King's Tower.

Keith had sold most of his furniture. Cardboard boxes squatted in the middle of the room and there was no desk, no chair. Francis made straight for the window, squeaking across the brown lino. He didn't want to notice how different everything felt. He didn't want to be interested.

Keith was sitting against a wall reading a paperback. He had looked up quizzically when Francis burst in, but immediately gone back to his book.

'I've come to say goodbye,' Francis announced. The grass below was threadbare with melting snow.

'I wondered whether I'd see you,' Keith said. 'I thought we'd had our little tiff and that was that. No more confidential chats.'

'I didn't come to see you, exactly.' Francis turned to face him. The bare room was so much larger than he expected, and so gauntly bright, he was dizzy for a second. There were a few dark scabs of sellotape on the walls, and a burst of drawing-pin holes where the desk had been.

'May I ask what you *are* doing here then?' Keith fastidiously turned down the corner of a page and closed his book.

'There were a few things I thought we ought to sort out. I mean, you're going and I thought we oughtn't to leave any . . .'

'Loose ends?' Keith interrupted. 'Well, I must say, old chap, that's really jolly decent of you. Really jolly decent.' He rested his chin in his hand and smiled up at Francis insolently. 'What you mean, of course, is that you don't want to go without telling me you found those pictures, and you want to know what I feel about that.' He paused, then barked, 'Isn't it?'

'I found them, yes,' Francis said. 'And I thought you might want to know what happened to them, because I . . .'

Keith solemnly held up one hand, palm outwards. 'I don't want to know. I don't care. I assume you didn't do anything stupid like show them to Rex or anyone, otherwise I'm sure I'd have heard. So I suppose you've destroyed them. Boiler, at a guess.' He smiled again, sourly, then slid the book into his pocket and stood up. 'Am I right? Or have you kept them for yourself? Some of them were rather good, and after all, Jamieson was your friend.'

Francis had rehearsed this scene dozens of times, but couldn't remember his lines. 'Well, at least you do me the courtesy of thinking I've destroyed them,' he said stiffly.

'Yes,' said Keith, slowly standing up, 'I do you that courtesy.'

'But what were you doing?' Francis was suddenly plaintive. 'I mean, what was the point?'

'Does there have to be a point?' Keith lounged against the wall, his deep relaxed voice was unruffled. In his dark suit, with the white wall behind him, he looked as if he were posing for a portrait.

'But you lied to me. You let me think you'd destroyed them.'

'So what? It didn't do you any harm.'

'But it was a lie!' Francis burst out. 'You were my friend and it was a lie! If you lied to me about that you might have lied to me about other things.'

'Oh?' Keith said, drawing the sound out superciliously. 'What sort of other things?'

'Anything.' Francis spoke to the bare wall. He knew he might as well have looked Keith in the eye and said, 'Catherine. Adele.'

'Anything, eh?'

'Well, what about Jamie then?'

'Jamie?' Keith repeated languidly. 'Oh, you mean that note thing. I never really thought I'd send it. In fact, I didn't even finish it, did I? No; I just wrote it to amuse myself, to let off steam. I thought it was a pretty bitchy thing he did, you know, and I was angry.' Keith smiled. 'Still, since it didn't get sent, no harm done there either.'

Francis pulled the magazine from under his arm.

'Brought your organ to show me, have you?' Keith asked, tilting his head and staring Francis in the groin. 'You've done a good job on it, I'll give you that. But I don't think I actually want to hear you read bits from it, if you don't mind. In fact, to be perfectly honest I'm going to have to tell you to piss off now. My people will be here in a moment, and I want to go and meet them.'

'You can't go yet. I haven't . . .'

'You haven't finished, have you?' Keith interrupted calmly again. 'Well this is still my place, you know, and I'm telling you: I *have* finished.'

156

Francis stamped his foot, but the sound was a puny thump, not the passionate crash he wanted. He blundered on regardless. 'It doesn't matter that you didn't do it. You thought of doing it, that's the point.' He paused; he could hear himself in the warm of Adele's car, saying: 'What I do isn't what I think about.' He thrust the magazine forward, shaking the open pages.

Keith bowed over them, as if he were examining the contents of a display case in a museum. 'I see,' he breathed at last. 'Or I think I see.' He dipped to the pages once more, then straightened. 'Yes, I do see. That silly little mystery photograph is me, isn't it? That's what you're telling me.' He sighed. 'I suppose you took it that night after I got stoned. I must confess, I was puzzled when I found the film had gone from my camera, but I decided you were just playing safe, making sure I hadn't got any more pictures on it for my file.'

'Your file? What do you mean, your file?'

'Oh, for Christ's sake, Frank,' Keith answered lazily. 'Surely you didn't think you and Jamieson were the only ones. I mean, I know I said I thought you were special, but . . .'

Francis gaped. 'But that's . . .'

Keith laughed. 'Blackmail? Surely you weren't going to say blackmail, were you? Christ, I do believe you were. Well, let me put you right about that, at least, my little cocky.' He bent close to Francis. 'I was keeping them because I liked them. Because I like looking at them. Got that? Remember how we used to feel? And I expect I'll keep them for the same reason. I can't tell when I might want to look at them, can I? Or why. I just can't tell.'

'I don't believe you,' Francis mumbled, struggling to keep his voice steady. 'I was giving you a taste of your own medicine!'

Keith pouted. 'I can understand how you worked that one out, Frank, really I can. But I'm sorry to tell you I just don't care. I think it's the most pathetic thing I've seen in my entire life. But of course that's your problem, isn't it, not mine.' His voice grew gradually louder. 'Don't you see? I'm leaving. I'm going. Now. In five minutes. And I don't care about this. Even if I thought you had the balls to tell anyone what that picture was – anyone who mattered – and I don't – well . . .' He took a deep breath and spoke softly again. 'It wouldn't matter. I won't be here. I'll have nothing to do with here. I'll be gone. Have you got that into your skull?'

'You deserved it!' Francis had meant to shout, but his words flapped on to the floor between them, graceless and cowering like fledgling birds.

Keith folded his arms. 'Poor old Frank. You still don't see, do you? Oh well, I don't suppose I can explain it now if I haven't managed already.' He was jaunty, almost affectionate. 'Oh well, oh well. I'll just go, then. Don't be here when I come back, will you, there's a good fellow.' The door opened and closed like an eye winking and he vanished.

Francis dropped the magazine and sank on to the nest of cardboard boxes. Below him on the drive people were greeting each other. A dog was barking, and a woman's laugh rolled brassily across the playing fields. None of it had anything to do with him. He looked round the room as if he were a prisoner inspecting a new cell. White walls, white ceiling, white sky filling the window, white light draped like dust-sheets over his clothes and skin. He rubbed his forehead. It ached enormously. He was tired; he wanted to curl up where nobody would disturb him. He wanted to go home to the brigadier's house and lie in the dark there, like Catherine had done.

The door flew open and Keith bulked above him. Francis was baffled. Keith had only just left – what was he doing back so soon? He winced up. 'I was just going, I . . .'

'I came back to see you, you fool.' Keith was glistening, and a stripe of his black hair was glued across his forehead like a splash of ink. He looks utterly different, Francis thought. He's only been gone a minute and he's changed completely.

Keith scooped the magazine off the floor and hurled it

against the wall; it fluttered and crashed. 'That piece of shit,' he shouted, his voice strangled. 'That's just contemptible. It's nothing.' He kicked the magazine and it scooted across the lino into the alcove where the red cushions had been. He strode after it, then suddenly flung up his arms and supported himself against the wall, head down, breathing heavily like an athlete after a race. When he turned to Francis again he had collected himself. He poked his fingers through his hair and began speaking carefully, arranging his words as if they were pieces of a jigsaw. 'OK, then. Let's go back to the beginning. Let's see if I can make you understand that way. I know you've had a difficult time, right? Very difficult, with Catherine and everything.'

'Don't patronize me.' Francis scrabbled to his feet and backed away. 'And don't bring Catherine into it.'

'Oh, but she must come into it; she must, she must,' Keith said in a cold seesaw. 'You see that, surely. You couldn't expect her to die and nothing to happen. Really, Frank. Don't be ridiculous.' He gave a wide smile. 'That's why I didn't mind about a few rows and things, you see. I expected it. I thought they might be good for you, even. That's why I let us have them, then let them blow over.'

'After London?' Francis pressed his shoulders against the hard cold wall. 'You didn't let that one blow over. I didn't let you. I didn't want to see you, and that's how it was. We didn't see each other. That's not what I call blowing over.'

'I told you not to be ridiculous, Frank. I'm talking about before that.'

'Rows before that?' Francis asked in a trivial voice that was not his own. 'I don't remember rows before that. What's happened to your wonderful sense of history?'

Keith darkened. 'Don't get sarcastic with me about history,' he said softly. 'I'm the one that knows about history, remember?'

Francis stuck his tongue into his cheek, poking his skin into a blunt pyramid. 'We seem to be getting rather off the point, don't we?'

'Off the point? Would you say so? I'd say not, actually. I'd say all these things tied up, only you can't see it.' Keith tilted his head back. 'At first I thought we were having rows because you were still upset about Catherine. Then I realized we were having them because you're just like that. You're like that all the time. You don't know what to do, so you do everything sort of secretly. Everything to do with your feelings, I mean. You do it half-heartedly. Like that fucking photo. Why didn't you insult me openly, if you wanted to insult me at all?' Keith opened his eyes wide, triumphantly. 'You don't know how to make things happen, Frank. You're obsolete – you know that? Right at the start of your life. Obsolete. You and all your lot.'

'What do you mean, my lot?' Francis asked wildly. 'You're one of us too. You're part of it.'

'I'm fucking not one of you.' Keith jabbed his forefinger at Francis, and held it quivering in front of his face. Then he folded his arms once more. 'I mean your father,' Keith said. 'That lot. My people aren't like your people. My people think. They talk. Even when we don't agree, we talk. We're alive! We do things! We don't just sit around blubbering about the past. I've seen your father, don't forget. Sitting in that big house in the country wondering what will become of it all. Paralysed. Not knowing what to do. Up to his ears in misery.'

'Don't talk like that about my father,' Francis whispered. He realized that he sounded like Adele and tightened his fists, pulling himself together. 'Anyway: what have *you* done? What have you done that I haven't? I'm just younger than you, that's all. I haven't even tried to do half the things you've done – I haven't had any chance yet.'

Keith put his hands on his hips, calm again. 'What have I done? Christ, Frank, I don't even know where to begin telling you. Let's just say I've got on with it, shall we, while we've been stuck here. And now Tariq . . .'

Francis nodded. 'Oh, you've heard from him at long last, have you?'

'Of course I've heard from him,' Keith said. 'We're meeting. You see what I mean? It's all beginning. You just sit here in a great puddle of shit. A great puddle. Pathetic. Just like your father.'

'I told you!' Francis hunched. 'Don't talk like that about my father. I don't have to be like that. I don't.'

'Oh?' Keith raised his eyebrows. 'So you agree with me, do you? I must say, I thought you probably would. But I have to tell you: if I want to talk like that about your father, I will.' He stepped closer. 'Once I thought you might be different. I thought you might escape – because of Adele, I suppose. But you're not different, and I'm fed up with waiting. There isn't time. You creep about. You suck up to me for ideas. You screw that tit Jamieson. You get all excited about O'Brien and his pathetic bombs. You piss around with Roberts. Don't you see? Whenever you actually try and do something, you fuck it up. You print that picture.' Keith was breathing hard again and his face had collapsed – the cheeks sunken, the wide mouth drawn back from his teeth.

Francis stared at the magazine in silence. Splayed on the lino, a few pages erect, it looked like a dead chicken. 'I don't see what's so different about lion's shit,' he said expressionlessly. 'If chucking that around was doing something, I don't see what's so great about doing.'

Keith waved one hand. 'It isn't the same.'

There was a second, longer silence, then Francis said, 'Anyway, I did do something that day in London. I joined in.'

Keith nodded slowly, taking his time. 'Funny, that. I never believed you did.' He laughed drily. 'I thought you were lying.'

'There was my picture,' Francis said. 'In the paper.'

'Ah, the famous picture. I can tell you, I looked at that picture and if it was you, well, you could have fooled me.' Keith sighed. 'No, to be honest I never did believe you about that. And to be equally honest, I never expected you to believe me.'

'What do you mean? About what?'

'About Adele. About me having seen her that day, and her sending you her love.'

Francis looked down. The brown skin of the lino was swarming with tiny cracks. It looked as though it needed oiling – except that it also looked smooth and supple, massaged by shoes coming and going. Keith's shoes and his own shoes.

'Anyone at home?' Keith tapped Francis painfully on the head with a stiff forefinger. 'The least I expected was for you to say you never believed me. Go on; why don't you say it? Though of course, even if what I've told you is true, even if I didn't see her, there's plenty of time. Plenty of time for me to see Adele if I want to, now that I'm free. I can do what I want.' He yanked open the door. 'What do you think about that, eh? Not that I can be bothered to wait and find out. Like I say; I've waited long enough.'

Sprightly voices soared up the stairs behind him.

'This is the juniors, here,' a boy was saying.

'How nice, darling,' a woman answered.

'It's great. I'll be here after Christmas. Next to Baynham.'

'Is that good?'

'Oh yes. He's very popular. It's great.'

'That's nice, darling.'

Their voices faded and Keith raised one hand. Francis had turned away, and caught him only in the corner of his eye, blurred and stretched like a figure in the margin of a television screen. 'Well, once more with feeling,' Keith said. 'I can't wait any longer. So perhaps you wouldn't mind pissing off at last. I hope we never see each other again, but I expect we shall.'

I can't hear him, Francis thought; he must be going downstairs on tiptoe. He reached the window and leant his forehead against the glass. He saw himself falling – or not himself, but someone else falling, indolently turning over and over with arms stretched wide. They used stunt men for that sort of thing in films. Or dolls. Not real people, anyway.

162

He smiled. He hadn't meant real people. He'd meant people who suffered. People whose story it was. They stepped aside at the last minute, real people, and someone else took over. It was called 'taking the fall'.

He closed his eyes. Catherine's name rolled into his head, and for no reason he could understand he thought of a stretch of river near the brigadier's house, at home. He hadn't been to the river for years – it was sullen and sinister, with scraggy bushes along the bank, and strands of fishing line tangled in them. The water was mahogany. As children, they'd been told about one particular fish there, which had sometimes been seen, but never caught. A hoary pike, shovel-faced, massively bearded. No one knew how long it had been snapping up small fry, lurking among weed, sinking like an ingot when on the brightest days a wan finger of sunlight melted into the depths. By now it must be huge. A giant.

Francis imagined the pike filling the river, too vastly long to turn, too deep-chested to stay hidden. He saw the mottled green and brown of its enormous sides glistening out of the water like the flanks of a ship, the dripping brutal head with its wolf's eye and snake's backward-slanting teeth, the creamy pulse in its throat. It had lived its life alone and for itself, devouring and terrorizing, and now it had outgrown its solitude and burst into the miserable air.

He opened his eyes. He couldn't stay any longer – Keith would be back. Keith who hoped never to see him again. And Adele – she would arrive soon, too. He stared across the grass. The snow grew thinner as he looked. Dimples appeared, and a few large scoops and scallops of green cleared like whole islands. He thought of himself running, and of Keith watching him, perhaps from this window. His strides lengthened and the ground flowed easily, dusted with snow at first, then lush with young shoots, then a puzzle of baked earth, then waterlogged, then dusted with snow and frost again. Behind him lay the ramshackle skeleton of empty buildings. Shutters were closed, electricity turned off, doors locked. In front of him was the wood, and soon he would be inside it. Soon no one would see him, and Catherine's freckled face, with its swirling tail of red hair, would thrash furiously up at him from the undergrowth.